HAUNTED

HAUNTED

Real-life Encounters with
Ghosts and Spirits

JAY ALANI with NEIL D'SILVA

EBURY
PRESS

An imprint of Penguin Random House

EBURY PRESS

USA | Canada | UK | Ireland | Australia
New Zealand | India | South Africa | China | Singapore

Ebury Press is part of the Penguin Random House group of companies
whose addresses can be found at global.penguinrandomhouse.com

Published by Penguin Random House India Pvt. Ltd
4th Floor, Capital Tower 1, MG Road,
Gurugram 122 002, Haryana, India

Penguin
Random House
India

First published in Ebury Press by Penguin Random House India 2019

10 9 8 7 6 5 4 3 2

The views and opinions expressed in this book are the authors' own and the facts
are as reported by them which have been verified to the extent possible, and the
publishers are not in any way liable for the same.

ISBN 9780143444695

Typeset in Adobe Garamond Pro by Manipal Technologies Limited, Manipal

Printed at Repro India Limited

www.penguin.co.in

To all the ghosts and gods out there.
And to every single person on this planet who believes in them.

Contents

Introduction

There is a world beyond what our eyes can see. This is the realm of the unknown, or what we have now come to call the paranormal. This world, we believe, coexists with ours. It is not on the fringes, as some believers claim, nor does it come alive only after the twilight hour. Rather, it is right here in our midst, interspersed with our elements, and even interacting with our world in ways we cannot truly fathom.

We owe our perception of the world to our five senses, but even these senses have their limitations. We can see only in a particular kind of light (approximately 380–740 nanometres) which we call the visible spectrum, and we can hear only a specific range of audio frequencies (20–20,000 hertz). We face similar limitations in our other senses too. Our taste buds can only understand the four basic tastes and their various combinations; our olfactory senses can only take in smells that stimulate the nasal cells; our skin can only feel tactile sensations if the contact is over and above a particular pressure. And yet we commit the grand fallacy of thinking that only what we can perceive is true and whatever we cannot perceive does not exist.

Our belief that the truth is limited to what we can perceive is, in reality, the falsest belief. There is a much larger world out there, one that eludes us for whatever reason, a subset of which is the realm of the paranormal.

Jay Alani has dedicated his life to finding the truth of this paranormal world. Born in Patna, Jay schooled in Darjeeling. It was in a hostel there, when he was not yet a teenager, that he had his first brush with the paranormal, an experience that has been detailed in one of the stories in this book. This episode put him on the path to seeking answers. Later, he moved to Bengaluru to complete his high school education and then studied mass communication in Delhi. Following a brief stint in Mumbai, he is presently working in Delhi.

Throughout his life's journey, Jay's interests have veered towards unearthing the truth of the paranormal world. He set out on his first exploration in 2015, and this whetted his appetite for many more ahead. Today, he travels all over the country to research and investigate haunted locations.

Through his varied pursuits, Jay has attempted, time and again, to reach out and discover if there is any access to spirit entities, to know whether they exist in the form we think. To date, he has visited hundreds of sites within India that have some kind of dubious reputation of being haunted, and through his keen sense and acumen, he has tried to learn about what lends these places their particular aura.

This book brings to you readers accounts of ten of his most hair-raising paranormal experiences, when he came close to finding out the truth about this unknown world. From noted haunted locations, such as the abandoned village of Kuldhara and the Bhangarh Fort, to relatively unheard-of places, such as Vas Villa in Bengaluru, Jay has bravely scoured every inch of these locations. The results of his encounters in these places are unpredictably varied.

This book is an attempt to understand whether these so-called haunted locations live up to their reputations. Do they harbour phenomena that human eyes cannot see? Is there any truth behind the tales that have arisen around these locations? Armed with a great deal of courage, Jay has spent entire nights in these places to come up with answers to these questions. *Haunted . . .* is a memoir of his experiences.

Chronicling Jay Alani's explorations for this book is popular horror author Neil D'Silva. While Jay provides the stories and experiences, Neil finds the words that form the narrative.

We hope this book will present the truth behind these infamous locations in our country and help people understand the paranormal world in a better light.

Jay Alani and Neil D'Silva

1

The Lost Child of Kuldhara

I, JAY ALANI, known to people as an investigator of the paranormal and all things mysterious, bring to you these stories culled from my experiences. These are my exploits in some of the most haunted places in India, some well-known and some shrouded in namelessness, and all of them guaranteed to make you see a side of our country that you have never experienced before. I begin this rollicking ride with my adventure at Kuldhara.

With all the legends and lore that revolve around the abandoned town of Kuldhara, it is a wonder that I did not visit it earlier than I did. This is a village in the Jaisalmer district of Rajasthan, established in the thirteenth century. Somewhere around 200 years ago, the people of this village vanished without a trace. No one knows where they went or the reason why they left. The mass exodus of people from Kuldhara and their subsequent disappearance remains an unexplained historical mystery. With no evidence available, strong local belief holds that it was because of a curse unleashed on them by a mystical foreigner. Today, the empty and barren Kuldhara attracts tourists, archaeologists, historical experts, as also a vast number of paranormal investigators.

My visit to Kuldhara happened by accident. That cold, fateful night, it was not my intention to be there, and I was caught unawares, ill-prepared. I made it out of the place safely, but the trip left me with memories for a lifetime. Journey with me as I recount the terrifying night that I spent at Kuldhara and the hair-raising experiences I had with a 'lost' child.

My visit to Kuldhara came about when a college friend invited me to his wedding in Jaisalmer. I was in Delhi then, and I drove down in my white Tata Safari. Accompanying me was a close college buddy who had also been invited, Rohan Achari. Jaisalmer is a historically rich city in the state of Rajasthan and is situated in the Thar desert. If you have been to the city, you will know that for miles around there is nothing but desert sand. Dotting the landscape are grand havelis and monuments. The people here are always colourfully dressed and display a great sense of joie de vivre. This is especially visible during the hugely famous Jaisalmer Desert Festival, which beautifully showcases Rajasthani folk music and dance, including the magnificent Kalbeliya and Ghoomar dances. Most of the local families here have inhabited the place for generations, resulting in a close-knit society where everyone knows everyone else.

The opulence of the wedding in the midst of such arid land bedazzled us. The venue was an ancestral haveli, and it was every bit the grand Rajasthani affair one would expect it to be. Music and dance pervaded the atmosphere of the place where royalty had once resided. The family of the groom were wealthy to the point of extravagance, and they left no stone unturned in the hospitality department. The entire haveli was bedecked with brilliant lights that one could see from miles afar. Sitting there, oblivious to the rest of the world outside, we felt like *baraatis* at a royal wedding of yore.

The event I am about to narrate took place on my first night in Jaisalmer, the night before the wedding. After dinner, Rohan and I were assigned to a room. It didn't look like we'd get any sleep that night though. With less than a day to go for the wedding, there was quite a bit of commotion all around, with the attendants looking after the last-minute arrangements in the halls outside. The two of us chatted for a while and then Rohan said, 'Come on, yaar, let's go out for a smoke.'

That sounded like a good idea. Cigarettes could help us pull through the cold night. But the closest shop was at the Jaisalmer railway station, 6 kilometres away.

Rohan was already at the door, wearing his jacket, stepping into his shoes.

'Come on, man! Don't you feel claustrophobic all cooped up like this?'

It was true. Despite the grandeur of the mansion, the rooms were quite small. Rohan knew about my career pursuits in the realm of the paranormal, but he only had a layperson's view of it. He had no idea that I had been in places far more claustrophobia-inducing than this—caves and tunnels and mines! In any case, I was here for a wedding.

I had no intention of raking up any talk about my mysterious career.

But he was tempting me now. So I put on my sweater, pulled up the hood and grabbed the keys to my Tata Safari. Slapping him on the back, I led him out.

We left the hubbub of the wedding haveli behind and got into the car. Only once I was out of the room did I realize what I had been missing. That lonely desert drive was invigorating to say the least. I was the one driving; Rohan provided the silent company I needed. Silences have been my long-time companions anyway, and this was the kind of rural solitude that could be both exhilarating and mind-numbing at the same time. Most people would kill for such pleasures.

We got our smokes outside the railway station and sat on a rickety bench. Puffing away into the night like that, there was no need or desire to look at the watch, but when I did, I shot up like a spring. It was nearing 1 a.m. The platform vendors had shut shop hours ago, and the only people at the station were the passengers waiting overnight on the platform for their early-morning outstation trains.

I prodded Rohan to get up. A yawn and a stretch and much reluctance later, we walked towards my car.

The return journey was not as silent. We had both loosened up a bit; maybe the smokes and the glimpses of routine civilization at the station (meaning people in non-wedding attire and without the beaming smiles of hospitality) did it for us. As we drove back chattily to the haveli, letting in the nocturnal breeze through the open windows, our voices were loud and we even hummed a few film songs. We would survive the wedding the following day, it appeared.

But destiny would force us to take a different route.

Rohan was in the middle of a bawdy song and I was laughing at his pathetic attempt to sing, when I spotted something ahead in our path and—

Screech! I stepped on the brakes with all my might.

There was a boy standing bang in the middle of the road.

He just stood there, without a care in the world, staring, his hair in disarray, his hands lying limply by his sides. But he looked pale, white as a ghost, as if numbed by shock. I thanked my lucky stars; the car had stopped just short of the spot he seemed rooted to.

To this day, I thank those reflexes. A fleeting moment of indecision, and I would have been guilty of killing a little boy in a road accident, something I would never have been able to live down afterwards.

'Wh-who is that?' Rohan asked, coming back to his senses.

Leaving his question unanswered, I opened the car door and rushed out to the boy, who was standing eerily still. Something was very wrong with him. Not caring about anything else now, least of all that I had been in a near miss, I ran to see if everything was all right with the lad.

He appeared to be about twelve, and was dressed in good clothes, the kind people from these parts might wear when they go somewhere special—a full-sleeved shirt and jeans. He had leather shoes on, and these were coated with dust, a sign that he had been walking quite a bit.

'Are you all right?' I asked him. 'Why are you standing in the middle of the road?'

I felt his hands. They were cold. Just a shade warmer than deathly cold.

'Come . . . sit . . .' I guided him to a flat stone by the roadside. 'Get some water, Rohan,' I called out urgently. When Rohan got the water, I grabbed it and sprinkled some on the boy's face. That seemed to help. A flicker of life shone in his eyes.

I shook his arm. 'Now tell me what happened. What's your name?'

'Aa . . . Aayush.' His voice was squeaky, like a girl's. It sounded odd coming from his mouth.

'Okay. Aayush. Where are your parents?'

'There somewhere . . .'

I looked in the direction he was pointing at. It was a byroad that led away from the main highway.

'What's there?'

'We had gone there . . . for a picnic,' he squeaked. 'Came in the day . . . and then . . . they got lost . . .'

'What do you mean *they* got lost?'

'Ma and Papa got lost.'

I looked at Rohan, whose face wore a sympathetic expression. Just imagine the plight of the little lost boy wandering alone in the desert in the night like that. That kind of thing shakes people up for good.

'When did you see them last?'

'Before evening. The sun was still up.'

'And you are just roaming around like this since then? Why didn't you tell anyone?'

I felt my voice rise out of concern, but the boy might have construed it as anger. His eyes began to glisten. A small tear rolled out.

'Oh, all right . . . I am sorry,' I said, my tone immediately mellower. 'Tell me where you last saw them.'

Rohan said, 'Jay, I think we should call the police.'

At the mention of the police, the boy visibly blanched. I put a reassuring hand on his shoulders.

'Yes, do that,' I told Rohan and then turned to Aayush. 'Don't worry, Aayush. The police will help you find your parents. Who knows, maybe your parents have already lodged a complaint and are waiting for you at the police station?'

Rohan used his phone; mine was back at the haveli, on charge. We sat in silence as Rohan attempted the call, but after several tries, he said, 'No one's answering.'

It was closing in on 2 a.m. The boy was looking desperately at me, and Rohan seemed clueless. Something had to be done. Seeing the helplessness writ large on both their faces, the hero in me came alive.

'I'll help you find your parents, don't worry,' I told the boy.

The boy looked up, his eyes piercing mine.

'How?' Rohan asked.

Ignoring him, I guided Aayush to the car. Rohan followed mutely. I put the headlights on and looked ahead at the path that led to the right, where the boy had pointed. It was like a dark tunnel leading into the unknown.

'Is this the way?' I asked.

'Yes,' the boy nodded.

I had gone about 10 metres ahead, when the headlights beamed on a road sign. Rohan saw the sign before I did, and the colour drained from his face.

'What is it, Rohan?'

And then it hit me.

The sign read—KULDHARA.

Kuldhara!

The abandoned ghost village of Rajasthan.

———

I had been to Kuldhara once before, but that was just a quick visit with my uncle and aunt way back in my boyhood days. I was living in Delhi at the time and had travelled here with them for some work in Jaisalmer. We hadn't stopped here, really. My uncle probably didn't know about the reputation of the place back then, or he chose not to tell me. Only in later years did I realize that the Kuldhara I had passed through was one of the most notorious haunted locations in the country.

Legend has it that Kuldhara was once a beautiful village in the desert, with detailed house plans and architecture that intrigues archaeologists even today. About 200 families lived in this village and managed their needs within its self-sustained habitat. It is believed that the people were content and lived in harmony with the neighbouring villages and also brought in a good amount of revenue by way of taxation for the kingdom.

But all their wealth and prosperity came to an abrupt end about 200 years ago.

There are many theories as to why that might have happened, but the most popular one tells of an outsider who visited this village and fell in love with a local girl. His love was profound, but the girl did not reciprocate. The man felt jilted. To add insult to injury, when the villagers got to know of the one-sided affair, they decreed that the man must be thrown out of the village.

But the villagers did not know that this strange man was a mystic with knowledge of the dark arts. By the time they realized this, it was too late. The mystic was already livid with rage. Hurt and deeply insulted, the mystic cursed the entire village.

There is no record of the exact nature of the curse. But soon after it had been pronounced, the village emptied out, almost overnight. Whatever that mystic had said was so terrifying that all the 200 families practically scurried out of the village with only the clothes they had on their bodies, leaving all their possessions behind. To this day, no one knows where the villagers went; none of them have ever been found. It is said that they perished in the vastness of the desert and the wayward sands swallowed them up.

Soon, Kuldhara attained the reputation of being one of the most dangerous places in the world. Horrific incidents have been noted here by stray visitors. People living in the vicinity speak of unexplained voices heard in the night, disembodied voices that aren't accompanied by human bodies. Many also speak of children seen in these parts, children who seem to vanish the moment they are approached. Such apparitions are too many to ignore, so much so that people now avoid the route as much as they can. Even among those of us who are interested in the occult, it is a widely accepted fact that this once-prosperous town is now a hotbed of paranormal activity.

———

Driving for about twenty minutes in the wilderness, we saw a colossal stone structure in the distance. As the headlights beamed on it, it glistened in contrast with the velvety dark of the night.

'Is it a fort?' Rohan asked.

I shook my head. 'It's the gate to Kuldhara.'

That huge archway of stone flanked by a wall with ancient windows did look like the gate of any fort. But I had seen it before. It was the entry point for the village of Kuldhara. When I had first seen it as a child, it had made me wonder what the folks here possibly owned that was so precious that they had to protect it with such a monstrosity. I realized only later that this gate wasn't present in the times of the legend; it had been built more recently by the Indian government to promote tourism. A board outside it proclaimed the name of Kuldhara along with a brief description. In the darkness, I could not read the words clearly. The boy was still looking at me petulantly and I realized this was not the time to be reading signboards.

'Was it here?' I asked him.

'Inside. More inside,' he said.

I revved the engine and moved forward. Rohan was looking on with great suspicion, but he was too stunned to say anything. I made a mental note to go easy on him; he was the kind that gets easily shocked.

No sooner did I drive in through the gate than everything changed drastically.

The first difference I noticed was that it was getting colder. It was a gradual drop in temperature, probably not noticeable to the others because the weather was already chilly. But from experience I knew that this wasn't any ordinary chill. It cut right through the skin and flesh into the bone.

Even the sounds were different here. When we had been on the other side of the gate, there were faint sounds of distant vehicles moving on the road and random ambient sounds of civilization. But here, inside, everything had come to an abrupt stop. All nocturnal sounds had faded away, not even the slightest murmur of distant desert insects could be heard. It was an unsettling feeling. We could see the moon and stars above us, but it was as if we were cruising along in a soundless tunnel.

'Ahead. Ahead. The village is ahead,' the boy said. 'Ma and Papa are there.'

Inadvertently, my hand touched the boy's, and I felt his bones trembling. I reassured him, 'Don't worry. We will find them.'

A dog barked somewhere and then chose to howl. A howl that pierced right through the eerie silence of the night.

'There seem to be some houses there.' I pointed ahead.

In the distance, we could make out the bare bones of some stone structures. They were still about a kilometre away. I drove on.

The atmosphere was filled with strangeness now, and though I did not spell it out to the other two, my senses were on edge. As we went deeper in, there was a strange rustling sound, like something moving in the foliage, but when I turned to look, I saw that there were no trees on either side of the road. Yet this sound constantly followed us as I drove. I don't know whether the others heard it; it is quite possible that only I picked it up due to the faculty for extrasensory perception that I seem to have developed over time.

My mental radar was on high alert now. Given all I had heard about the place, I did not want to ignore any of the signs.

There were indeed houses arranged in a cluster-like formation. In some bygone era, this might have been a neighbourhood.

Aayush pointed at a house. I parked the car right outside it and stepped out.

'You have to be careful, guys,' I said.

'Of?'

'These are desert lands. They are infested with snakes and scorpions. They hide in the sand in the daytime, but at night, they are on the prowl.'

In my experience, during most paranormal tours conducted in desolate locations, ghosts are the least of the problems. The bigger problems are posed by living creatures who do not wish to be disturbed in what they consider to be their domain.

The house was a mere enclosure of walls without a roof. Even the walls stood only halfway up, a good bit having crumbled away over time. Before stepping into the house, I decided to equip myself. I always have some of my stuff handy, and for this one I went back to the car and got my infrared thermometer and K2 meter.

Rohan and Aayush held their breath as they eyed the items.

'Is this your ghost-hunting stuff?' Rohan asked.

I nodded.

'Why do you need it here? Do you think there are ghosts here?'

I did not want to say much; Rohan was clearly getting jittery. 'I am just intrigued,' I said.

He pointed at the infrared thermometer. 'Okay, tell me, what does this stuff do?'

I am always interested when someone asks me about my equipment. But time was of the essence at this juncture, so I decided to keep it brief.

'This one here is an infrared thermometer. It's like a normal thermometer, but with this one you have to point at the spot where you want to measure the temperature. Temperatures of surroundings are fairly constant, but if the temperature dips significantly, there might be something out of the ordinary there. Spectral beings give rise to what are known as cold spots.'

His expression was one of fascination mixed with fear. 'And this one?' He cocked an index finger at the K2 meter.

'This is a K2 meter. It's a modified EMF meter. EMF, as your physics knowledge must tell you, is electromagnetic frequency. See these five lights on it? The first light is always on since the earth itself has an EMF. But in the presence of stray electromagnetic fields, more lights light up depending on how strong the field is.'

'Oh, so you mean . . . ghosts cause an EMF too?'

'To be more accurate, ghosts can cause a shift in the electromagnetic frequency of the place.' I stuffed the devices in my pocket. 'But don't worry too much about them, I don't set much stock by these devices. It's just good to carry them sometimes. You never know.'

'So what will you do if there are ghosts here?' There was a faint but noticeable break in his voice.

'Don't worry!' I smiled at him. 'Ghosts aren't all evil! And the chances of finding something are very, very slim. Just that this is such an old place and is claimed to be haunted. And, after all, this is what I do, you know! You don't need to be afraid.'

As I pointed the thermometer at the house and strode ahead, I almost let out a gasp. The numerical reading changed rapidly as I moved closer. Temperature variations usually occur, but this wasn't just a small dip. When we came to what could have been the door of the house, the temperature was 5 degrees lower than what it was outside. My worst fears were beginning to get confirmed. Such a sudden lowering of temperature could never amount to anything good.

I addressed the boy. 'Show me the exact spot where you saw your parents last.'

Aayush stood still for a while and turned his head for a panoramic sweep of the place, as if to get a sense of direction. He scanned through all the other houses around. I could understand why he'd be confused. Everywhere we could see, there were broken structures of stone. They might once have been basic, four-walled homes with narrow doors and small windows. The windows were different, in that they were set higher than what we see in our modern homes. Such architecture was perhaps intended to keep the heat of the desert winds out.

One striking feature common to all the houses was the absence of a roof. It could be that the roofs had fallen with time, but from what I could tell, it appeared as if the roofs had never been constructed in the first place. Maybe the inhabitants of Kuldhara had some valid reason for not building roofs, and somehow that could tie in with the reason for their mysterious disappearance. But, like everything else about Kuldhara, this is a mystery that will never be resolved now.

My musings were interrupted when Aayush screamed out, 'That's the place!'

He was looking at a kind of alley between two broken buildings. We could see the path from where we stood, but the rest of it up ahead lay shrouded in total darkness.

'A-are you sure?' Rohan asked, his voice now a quiver. 'Let me try calling the police again . . .'

For some reason, I have never felt fear. That emotion is just not there in me. My friends tell me this is a bad thing, and my science professor once told me that a lack of fear can be harmful, as fear helps us to develop a sense of danger. But I cannot help it. Just as some people cannot get angry or excited, I do not get frightened. It's just the way I am made.

But that's not to say that I don't *understand* fear. In that moment, it was plainly obvious to me that Rohan was mortally petrified. The whole episode had been driving him nuts from the very start, and I could not ignore it any further.

'You go sit in the car if you wish, Rohan,' I told him. 'I'll go along that path and explore.'

'No!' he pleaded. 'I'd rather be with you than alone.'

'Are you sure?'

'Yes. Please don't leave me alone in this place. Let's just go back. Let's deposit this child at the police station. It's not our job.'

I looked him squarely in the eye.

'I know how to deal with anything, Rohan. *Anything*, you understand? Nothing will happen to us. But I am afraid for you. You might not be able to take it. Such things are unpredictable. That's why I ask you to go back to the car.'

'Are there ghosts here?'

I looked at the crazy readings on my infrared thermometer. 'I don't know.'

'Oh my God! Now you tell me you don't know!'

'Rohan . . . what do you wish to do? I want to explore this place now, and trust me, it will be safe.'

'I . . . I will come with you,' he managed, after a long pause. 'No, I don't want to go and sit in the car all alone. I am coming with you.'

'Then, come,' I said, patting him on the shoulder gently. 'I will make sure we do this as safely as possible.' I turned to the boy. 'Lead on, son,' I told him.

The boy went ahead of us. It was curious how he walked on, undaunted, not in the least bit hesitant. Just like that, he ambled into the darkness, seemingly oblivious to the creepy howling in the distance and the rustling of unseen leaves. How was he so unafraid?

The boy's fearlessness was not lost on Rohan. 'How much do you trust him?' he asked. 'Why would his parents come to such a creepy place at all?'

We were about ten steps behind the boy; he couldn't hear us. 'I don't know,' I said.

Truth is, the thought had entered my mind that the boy might not be a 'boy' after all. I'd not be surprised if this entire night turned into one of those supernatural moments you talk about till you die. For a while now, I admit, the boy had been striking me as a bit strange. There was something in his appearance, his gait and simply the manner of his being that seemed totally off. What if the boy was something else, not even human?

There is this case of a man from Delhi who claimed to have lived with his girlfriend for several days after she had died in a road accident. He hadn't heard of her death. They ate together, slept together and even made love. It was five days later when the police knocked at his door for an investigation into the girl's death that he came to know she had died. The 'girl', who was still in the inner room when he answered the door, vanished after that, and the man has not been the same ever since.

The boy could be anything that had developed a humanlike body, speech and even emotion. Such things are not completely out of the realm of possibility. They are known to happen.

'Whatever it is about him, I will know how to deal with it,' I assured Rohan.

Rohan either trusted me implicitly at that point, or he had no choice but to do so. We were too far in now for him to turn back alone. He kept close to me.

Meanwhile, I took out the K2 meter. Rohan eyed it suspiciously.

'Here it is!' Aayush suddenly exclaimed. 'This is exactly where we were this afternoon.'

I caught up with the boy and looked around. The EMF light was still in the normal zone, but the atmosphere had changed. The air was different here, musty to an extent. Not the clean desert air with the faint smell of silica in it; this smell was closer to that of rotting vegetables.

'What's that smell?' Rohan asked.

I wished I had an odour meter. I wanted to check if it was sulphur. Spirits are known to leave traces of sulphur wherever they go. I had to rely on my olfactory senses, and they told me it was sulphur.

'Relax,' I told Rohan for about the tenth time.

I panned the beam of my flashlight all the way around the walls of the house and up the ceiling. Then I noticed the other strange thing. This house had a roof.

That didn't go with the Kuldhara tradition of building roofless houses that I had seen so far. I moved around a bit. Rohan followed me closely, his toes bumping into my heels more than once. I noticed the faint traces of age-old paintings on the walls, felt the floor, which was better laid out than what we had seen in the other houses. I even found a drain in one of the corners, which had probably been the bathroom of the house at some point.

'This house is different from the others,' I remarked. 'I think this was their mukhiya's house or something.'

'Mukhiya?' Rohan asked.

'Headman of the village.'

The boy shouted again, and this time it startled me too. 'Here!' he yelled. 'See this.'

I quickly directed the flashlight at the spot. Plastic wrappers of biscuits and other snacks lay strewn about. Freshly opened ones, it looked like. There was even a half-eaten sandwich and the slice of bread was still fresh.

'This is exactly where we were picnicking,' Aayush said, his eyes twinkling.

'He speaks the truth then,' Rohan said. 'These are freshly opened packets.'

I said nothing. We were dealing with spirits here. Sourcing half-eaten fresh food from somewhere is not impossible for some of the naughtier entities of the spirit world. I poked at them and was suddenly assailed by a strong whiff of sulphur. This was totally out of place.

Now, I had to act cautiously. If this boy was indeed something else and not human, we had already been lured into his domain. Getting out of here would be tricky, and I had Rohan with me to take care of. My next steps would have to be taken with great caution.

I looked at the boy and said, 'Aayush, you don't worry. I will go look for your parents. If they are here, one quick tour of this place should help me locate them.' As I uttered the words,

I noticed that the boy didn't have a worried expression any more. Instead, he had a smile that stretched from ear to ear.

Quickly turning to Rohan, I said, 'I don't want you to follow me now. You have to go back.'

'But . . .'

'Go back, Rohan!' I said sternly.

'May I go to the car too?' The boy's tinny whimper was back.

I gave him a sharp glance. This was unexpected. 'Why do you want to go back? Don't you want to find your parents?'

'Please . . . I am tired!'

I quickly weighed the options. Rohan could not accompany me hereon, that much was clear. But I could not send Aayush with him either. Rohan was vulnerable and probably the 'child' had sensed that. The more I looked into the child's eyes, the more I was sure that there was something going on that was way beyond normal.

'I will not go to the car!' Rohan said then, and this time more adamantly. 'You leave all this and come back. Let's get out of here.'

And then, breaking the impasse between us, his phone rang. He looked at the screen and showed it to me.

The boy chimed in, 'Who is it?'

Rohan answered the call. He spoke for a minute. When he disconnected, his eyes were shining too. 'It was the Jaisalmer police,' he told the boy. 'Your parents aren't at the station. No complaints have been lodged. But the police are sending a team here to look. It seems they are taking all missing person complaints around Kuldhara seriously.'

'That's great,' I said. 'Now, before the police arrive, let me take a quick look at this house.'

I proceeded to explore the house. All my focus was now on the path ahead and the changes in my devices. The fact that I was actually in the heart of Kuldhara, one of India's most haunted locations, hit me hard only now.

I walked into the inner chambers of the house with apprehensions in my mind but no fear. However, I won't deny that I was beset by an overwhelming sense of curiosity, and that only heightened with each step I took.

Wanting to make the most of the few minutes I had left here, I stepped on, not realizing when I left Rohan and Aayush behind.

———

The house was plunged in darkness. I found myself in an inner room that had no windows. I couldn't fathom why anyone would design a room like that, that too in the middle of the desert where one welcomes whatever little breeze they can get.

I shone my light at the walls. There were a few cracks, telltale signs of the history of the place. They were stone walls, so the cracks weren't too deep or threatening. But they were there all the same.

One thing I noticed right away was the complete absence of cobwebs and dust. I would have thought a home left unoccupied for such a long period would have had huge streamers of cobwebs falling from the ceiling. There should have been inches of dust caking the walls. But, no, nothing like that. The room looked as if it had been swept clean just that morning.

Another big indicator of something sinister afoot.

As I held my K2 meter aloft, I noticed the second light blinking intermittently.

My steps fell slower and softer now. I began looking for another door to exit the room. There should have been one, as the entire house seemed to be structured in the form of a maze, with one room leading to the other.

But before I could pan my light to the far corner, I felt something cold and metallic poke beneath my feet, and I stumbled and fell.

Intrigue hit me before the physical ache.

I sat up on the floor immediately, not wanting to stay prone in that vulnerable position for long. Like a martial arts pro, I sprang up and assumed a fighting stance. What was it that had made me trip when I was being so careful?

My flashlight, which was now rolling a few feet away, revealed the portion of the floor where I had tripped.

There was a wooden door set into the floor! Its round brass handle was what had caught my foot.

Angry with myself for blaming spirits when the reason for my fall was something so physical and real, I grabbed the handle. What was down there? A room? A tunnel? A secret chamber?

It was quite a task to prise the door open. It seemed to weigh several hundred kilograms! Involuntarily letting out a loud grunt and ripping part of my shirt in the process, I managed to hoist the door open.

A dark hole lay exposed in front of me, dark as the insides of a grave that has lain untouched for centuries.

I directed my torchlight in.

And then I saw—

Eyes!

Red-and-brown eyes, perfectly round as marbles, all looking at me, hundreds upon hundreds of them.

What in hell's name was that?

It took me a moment to figure out what they were, and when I did, it was too late.

Bats!

Who knows how long those bats had been sleeping upside-down in that dingy underground chamber, undisturbed by man or nature!

The sudden shaft of bright light trained on them naturally angered them, and they broke into an unholy screech. I knew I had to get away on the double, but this time my reflexes failed me.

I heard the flapping of their wings with a dreadful sinking feeling in my heart, before I fell backwards on the floor, my head hitting the surface first, as the angry creatures whooshed up in a frenzy and flew out of the tiny recess in the wall.

I bore the scratch marks of their claws on my face and neck for a long time. One of the angrier ones even sliced my palm, and I had to seek medical attention for that later.

———

That underground chamber was a false alarm. When I came back to my senses, I saw what it was—a place to store foodgrain, perhaps wheat or jowar in those times. Desert folks did it to save the delicate grain from the intense heat; underground, it's always cooler.

About a minute later, when I had just about tied my handkerchief to staunch my bleeding palm, I heard Rohan's shrill scream.

'Jay! Jay! Come here quickly!'

It was coming from the main hall, and suddenly realizing that Rohan and Aayush were not with me, I made a quick dash in that direction. In those few quick paces, I confess, I felt an inexplicable terror. That boy Aayush was with him. Had something happened?

But the real scene was something different.

Rohan was still in the main hall. The moment I saw him, he hushed me into silence. The boy was standing next to him, equally paralysed.

'What is it?' I asked.

'Shh!' he whispered. 'Listen.'

In the pin-drop silence that prevailed now, I listened. And then it became audible—the sound of crying.

'Who is t—'

My question was cut off by Aayush. 'It's that girl.'

'Girl?'

The voice went on now, loud and clear. It was the distinct sound of a girl weeping, sobs and sniffles. No, it wasn't the voice of an infant. This sounded more like a grown-up girl, a teenager at least.

'Which girl?' I asked again.

'There was a girl outside,' Aayush said. 'I saw her when I was looking for my parents.'

'How did she look?'

'Young. Bigger than me, but young. But . . .'

'But what?'

'She was dressed in old and dirty clothes.'

'Did she tell you anything?'

'No.' Aayush shook his head. 'I asked her who she was and whether she had seen my parents. But she just kept on walking.'

'Okay, listen,' I told the two, even as the weeping voice began to rise in tenor. 'Look at my K2 meter. See the lights blinking?' Four lights were blinking now, when held in the direction of the sobbing sounds. 'That's not good.'

'What does that mean?' Rohan mumbled, almost out of breath.

A fifth light came on. All five lights on the K2 meter were lit up!

'Go back. Go back, Rohan. Go to the car.'

'What about me?' the boy asked. There was some kind of glint in his eyes that I did not want to look at directly.

As the lights stayed steady, the sound of the crying seemed to draw closer.

'That smell . . .' Rohan said.

The smell had aggravated by now. It was not rotten vegetables though. It was worse. It was rotten eggs. Sulphur.

'Get out!' I screamed. 'Rohan, go to the car. Go right out!'

'What about you?'

25

'I am following right behind you,' I said, grabbing the boy by his hand. 'I just need to make sure . . .'

'What?'

I didn't tell him. But I wanted to know if this spirit was malevolent. If it was, I needed to contain it somehow. Kuldhara was not a lonely place any longer, and roaming tourists and wandering spirits are never a good mix.

'Go!'

With that vehement ultimatum from me, Rohan broke into a run and headed out through the door. At the same time, I heard something crash behind me.

I wheeled around; there was nothing I could see. But the electric field was so high at this spot that I felt my hair standing on end, and this despite the fact that I wasn't really frightened. Maybe my hair was just responding to the high electric field caused by whatever entity was moving towards me.

'Who are you?' I asked aloud of the space in front of me, taking a tentative step backwards.

I heard nothing, and neither did I intend to. One of the tricks we ghost hunters use is to engage in direct conversation with spirits. If the spirit is not malevolent, it will back off at that, and even if it is, our forthrightness in addressing it throws it out of gear.

Behind me, I could sense that Rohan had reached the parking lot. He had my keys with him. I noticed that I was still holding Aayush by his arm. He had started to cry. For a moment, I wanted to release him and let him go with Rohan, but I was not sure what he was. He could have been possessed, for all I knew.

'Go back,' I spoke into the empty space that was causing the disturbance. 'There is nothing for you here. We are not here to trouble you in any way.'

And then Rohan screamed again.

The EMF field suddenly went back to normal. The blinking of the lights stopped.

I was completely confused as to what was going on, but a moment later, I got my answer.

The door of my car flew open all by itself and the headlights came on. That was what had made Rohan yell out, because the keys were still in his pocket.

'Jay!' he bellowed, and I ran out, dragging Aayush with me.

The headlights were blinking. A strong wind began to blow in the distance and the scattered sand threatened to sting my eyes. Shielding my eyes, I managed to reach the car, and just as I did, the headlights turned off.

'The door . . . door . . . It opened by itself.' Rohan's words came out in a tumble. 'I swear . . . I didn't touch . . .'

'It's all right. Just back off . . .' I said.

'What is it?'

I threw a sideways glance at the boy. No, he wasn't scared. There was not the slightest shade of fear in his expression. His crying had stopped too.

'Let's get into the car and go now,' I told him.

Rohan handed me the keys with the happiness of a prisoner being released after a long incarceration.

The moment I took the keys, the girl's weeping voice rang in our ears again.

Aayush smiled.

He actually smiled!

'Do you know who the girl is, Aayush?' I asked sternly.

'Forget that!' Rohan tugged at my arm. 'Let's go back. We have disturbed a lot of things here.'

Yes, I had to. Seeing the state Rohan was in, I knew he could have collapsed any minute. I took the boy firmly by the hand and got into the car. But I checked the insides first. Only once I was sure the car was safe did I ask them to get inside.

The voice rose in pitch behind us, and as I stepped on the accelerator, the wailing seemed to follow us. Rohan did not respond to it now, and I wondered if I was the only one hearing it.

———

With the tyres blazing on the dusty road, the silence of the night was shattered. The wails were still on my mind, if not in my ears, and I knew if I slowed down, there'd be more to come. We were still in the ghost town anyway.

The gate of Kuldhara was about a quarter of a mile ahead, and there was nothing to say right now. We just needed to get out of there.

With the exit in clear sight now, Aayush screamed.

'Papa!'

———

Rohan and I turned to see a couple standing to the left of the gate. In a burst of enthusiasm, Aayush slapped the back of my hand that was on the gear handle and said, 'My parents!'

I brought the car to a halt inches away from the two figures.

The boy, who had been perched on Rohan's lap so far, hopped over him, stepping on his toes in his excitement. He opened the door on his side and jumped out to meet his folks.

I stepped out too to witness the reunion. Then, giving them a piece of my mind, I asked where they had been the whole day.

'Just here. Looking for Aayush,' said the father.

'Is this the place to be?' I could hear my voice climbing an octave higher once again. For someone who perceives dangers that others simply cannot see, my anger was justified. But when I took another look at the simple rustic couple, I softened. 'Well, okay. As long as you have found your son, it's all good.'

The father joined his hands together in a gesture of gratitude. I realized I was some kind of saviour in their eyes, for having protected their son. And in that moment, I felt guilty for having apprehensions about the child. He was just an ordinary boy, after all, lost and separated from his parents, and lost in such a spooky place, no less.

Just as I was about to leave, the father asked me, 'What about the girl?'

It felt as if a cold slap had landed on my bare back.

'What girl?'

'The one who was roaming the Kuldhara streets,' he said. 'We asked her to come with us, but she didn't listen. She ran away somewhere and . . . we did not see her again.'

'Did you really see a girl?'

'Yes. There was this girl about fourteen or fifteen years old. Wearing village clothes. She seemed to be from these parts. When we told her that our boy was missing, she just nodded and continued walking ahead, as if she knew where our Aayush was. But it was difficult to keep up with her. She would turn around corners, and when we caught up with her, she would disappear. And then appear again a little ahead. This hide-and-seek went on for a long time. But we want to thank her. She led us here. Right where we found Aayush.'

'You are lucky, the whole lot of you,' I said with some feeling.

'Why, sir?'

'You won't understand. But now get out of here as soon as you can.'

In the distance, we saw headlights approaching. The police jeep was arriving. We walked ahead and stopped by the vehicle which came to a halt.

'What are you boys doing here?' a constable shouted, even before he stepped out of the vehicle.

'We were just—' Rohan began.

'Don't you know how dangerous this place is?'

We nodded. 'We met a lost boy who said his parents were here. We were just trying to find his parents,' I explained.

'We received the call,' the constable said. 'Where is the boy now?'

Smiling happily, I said, 'We just found his parents. They took him. Look, right there behind—'

But I froze mid-sentence. For as I turned and pointed in the direction where we had just met the boy's parents, I realized there was no one now. Nothing at all! Just an empty stretch of land that led to the village of Kuldhara beyond.

The constable probably noticed my finger trembling. His tone was kinder when he spoke again.

'You are lucky. Others have not been so lucky.'

'But . . . but . . .' Rohan stuttered. 'Didn't you come here to locate the boy's parents too?'

'Fools!' the constable roared. 'Don't you see? There's no boy here. No parents. We came to rescue *you*! We have lost count of how many foolish young people like you have come here looking for adventure and then never been found. Just go away now and stay out of here.'

I was speechless. Still staring into that empty space, I could not imagine how close I had been to otherworldly people and yet not realized it. If Rohan hadn't been with me, I'd not have believed that night had ever happened.

––––––––

Come to think of it, that night I really got lucky. I was saved because I played safe and didn't trigger the spirits much. I didn't have the foggiest clue that I would end up in what is touted to be one of the most haunted spots in the world, let alone in India. I could easily have met my end the way some paranormal researchers have at this very spot.

Rohan was in grave danger, though he did not know it at the time. Negative energies always feed on fear, and that night, Rohan was a bundle of fear. If I hadn't been there, he would not have made it out unscathed.

And who was the boy Aayush in reality? How could he have been so real, so much like any other boy? In fact, if it weren't for the fact that he and his parents had done the disappearing act right in front of our eyes, we'd have argued with the police further.

Who was he in real life? Perhaps he was once alive and had visited the place with his parents. Perhaps they had died there, or been possessed and unaware of it. And if I hadn't been cautious, maybe I too would have been roaming eternally in Kuldhara village.

But what stayed with me is what I saw in Aayush's eyes. When he held his father's hand and we proceeded towards the police jeep, I looked back at him once to wave goodbye and found him staring at me. He gave me a curious look then, and in that look I saw something that I have never seen in the eyes of anyone else. It is an inexplicable, discomfiting feeling that will never leave me. To this day, I lose sleep on some nights thinking that that boy is still out there, walking endlessly with his parents without knowing who they really are.

2

The Voice in the Hostel

IT IS DIFFICULT to explain why I got into paranormal investigation. Why does the other world fascinate me so much? To be honest, there is no straightforward answer to that question. Why does one choose a particular career? It is usually a cumulation of events that leads us on the road we travel. However, most of us recall that one defining moment that started it all. It is termed variously as an 'epiphany' or 'the calling', and it occurs but once in everyone's lives. Those who heed it find the path they are meant to take.

Such an epiphany happened in my life too—quite early on, in fact. I was still a schoolboy in a hostel in Darjeeling when I was subjected to a terrible experience. Here I recount that life-changing incident that brought me to where I am today.

I am frequently asked about what triggered my foray into this dark and often dangerous field of paranormal investigation. The popular notion is that no one enters such a domain of their own volition; there has to be some precipitating factor that pushes them into it. To be honest, I never made a conscious decision with regard to it. However, certain events that transpired in my life left their indelible influence on me, which led me on this path. In retrospect, there is this one particularly terrifying incident that stands out from my childhood, which might be the reason why I am here.

This fateful incident occurred when I was all of eleven years, a student of class five in a school far away from my home, in Darjeeling, and I lived in the hostel attached to it.

This school (which I shall not name) was situated on a plain plot of land in the hill station. The unique thing about it was that it had a stretch of forest area behind it and another in front of it. The approach road to the hostel was through the forest, and for all practical purposes, it was cut off from the rest of the world. In this hostel, we lived in dormitories, or dorms, as we call it, eighteen boys to each dorm; and we followed the strict regimen that is observed in all hostels.

One of the highlights of my education in that boarding school was the sports. The prime focus was on football, which we would practise on the grounds up to 5.30 p.m. At dusk, we would take a break and then walk back to our hostel. Our dinner was in the main hall of the hostel from 8–9 p.m., after which we would return to our dorms. We would fool around a bit and then head to our bunk beds, nine per dorm. There was a strict policy of lights out at eleven, and after gossiping a bit in the darkness, we'd invariably fall into our much-earned sleep of the day.

All of us, except Ashish Yadav.

Like us, Ashish was also in the same class, but he looked much older. To begin with, he was at least one head taller than the rest of us and had the musculature of an older boy. You could easily spot him in a crowd of other fifth-graders, and even some of the eighth-graders for that matter.

Ashish loved sports. Perhaps his physique led the way and he developed a passion for sports. He was great at football, and seeing his potential, our PT instructor, Barua sir, got him into basketball practice as well. This made his schedule different from ours. While the rest of us got free from the sports field at dusk, Ashish continued till 8 p.m. for basketball practice with the other older boys from the higher classes. Given his nature, this was great fun for him, for he was quite at home with everybody. Within a few days, he had made friends with everyone on the senior team, and even in the main hall, we could hear frenzied shouts from the field outside—'Ashish, pass the ball!', 'Ashish, cover me!' and occasionally 'Ashish just scored a goal!'

Ashish was also full of strange habits. Due to his schedule, he was always the last person to walk in for dinner. And he did that with swag, enjoying the attention, calling out everyone's names as he passed them. Heads naturally turned in his direction. Everyone wanted him at their table. But Ashish's table was always reserved—it was the one where his close buddies sat, and that included me.

This weird behaviour would continue after lights out. There were many nights when we'd be rudely awakened by him at odd hours. He'd come right up to where we lay, shake us brusquely, call out our names and whisper in our ears that he wasn't getting any sleep. Whenever that happened, there was nothing to do but wake up and chat with him in the darkness. But again, we never complained about these nocturnal sit-throughs. Ashish would regale us with his stories, which were about his triumphs on the football field and basketball ground, and how he wanted to see the world around the school premises. Regardless of how zonked we were, sleep would always vanish after listening to his exploits.

So that was Ashish, our erratic and slightly eccentric friend, but one whom we were so enamoured by that I dare say every boy in the school might have wanted to be in his shoes at some point or the other.

And then, one morning, no one wanted to be Ashish Yadav. Ever.

———

I remember that night vividly. It was a biting cold November night and our term exams were just around the corner. There was a different atmosphere in the school as these were important exams, and even the biggest troublemakers would think twice before taking them lightly.

That night, we were in the hall and already halfway through dinner when we noticed that Ashish hadn't returned from basketball practice.

He had been playing basketball for three months then, and there wasn't a single night when he hadn't come to the main hall directly after practice. At first, we did not think much of his absence, but then I saw some of the teachers rushing hurriedly through the halls, looking for someone. Just like that, my hair stood on end.

I pointed out Ashish's absence to my other dorm friends—Tabish and Ananya. When it hit them, they sat bolt upright and then there was no peace.

News shortly trickled down to us that Ashish was missing. The basketball players had all returned, but he wasn't with them. Someone from the team informed the teachers that Ashish had asked them to carry on, saying that he'd follow close behind, but he had never turned up.

The entire hostel spilled out on to the field that night. Lights out was forgotten. The teachers were busy looking everywhere. Even our principal, Mr Shastri, was out, enveloped in his many sweaters. Every nook and cranny of the hostel, the campus, the school building and the whole field was thoroughly scanned. We returned to our dorms at around 2 a.m., and the last thing we heard was that two of our teachers had left for the police station to lodge a missing person complaint.

Ashish was found the following morning.

Rather, his corpse was found, tragically positioned, face down, in the shrubbery of the forest area that bordered the playing grounds.

———

The entire school was immediately plunged in gloom.

That day when we received the news, it was like everything came to a standstill. Everyone, including the teachers, spoke in hushed whispers even when no one else was around. The warden did not come out of his room at all, and the resident teachers, peons and basketball players were all rounded up throughout the day for investigations. We boys were told not to leave our dorms, but we could see the police in the grounds, and Principal Shastri was in a state that we had never seen him in before.

The most gut-wrenching moment came when Ashish's parents arrived to claim the body. His father slapped his forehead in utter resignation and collapsed on the ground, and his mother let out a wail that echoed through the air. The teachers tried to hold her back, but she had gone insane in her grief, beating her chest, trying to escape the grip of the teachers as if she wanted to run somewhere far away from this heartbreaking news.

The despairing sight of it all—I had never seen anything like that before in my life, nor have I since.

It shook us all up. Not a single word was spoken throughout the day. Though we were not called upon to mourn, we were silent participants in the grief that had suddenly spread all over.

Three days later, Principal Shastri found the necessity (and perhaps the courage) to address the rest of us boys and apprise us on what was going on. Some preliminary findings of the investigation had been shared with him, and he decided to let us in on the details. I still remember his short speech, word for word.

'Boys,' he said, 'this is a moment of profound grief for all of us. Despite our best precautions, a great tragedy has befallen us, and there is nothing we can do. We will all miss Ashish greatly, and given the kind of boy he was, most of us will miss him for a lifetime. I feel we all need to have some kind of closure on what transpired that night. According to the police, Ashish had strayed into the forest for some reason. We do not know if he went there of his own will or if something forced him or enticed him to do so. The police surmise that, due to the uneven path of the forest and the darkness that had set in, Ashish had an unfortunate fall. As he fell, his head hit a rock jutting out from the ground, and that is what proved fatal, as the forensic reports suggest. Blood was found on the rock and there was a wound on his forehead. I hereby advise all students to avoid the forest altogether, and strict rules will apply to anyone who flouts this warning.'

The speech numbed us. How strange life is! Ashish, the strongest of us all, lost his life so early and that too to such a nasty quirk of fate. A fall! Was that the way for a boy like Ashish to go?

None of us ever blamed the school. It was no fault of theirs, for the boarding school and the hostel were both very particular about being vigilant and ensuring the safety of the students. In fact, mere days after the tragedy, the school built a wall separating the forest area from the sports ground and made it all the more impenetrable for anyone who might want to venture in.

———

Two weeks later, our exams began.

As the daily grind took over, memories of the tragic incident began to phase out from most students' minds. I too was engrossed in my studies, for the importance of the term exams had been hammered into the heads of all students quite incessantly. It was on the night of the first exam that something happened that put me on edge.

It was around half past midnight. I was the only one up in my dorm, studying for the next day's paper. Our dorm accommodated eighteen boys who slept on nine bunk beds. Tabish and I shared a bunk bed, with me sleeping on the upper one. Our bed was the closest to the door. Each bunk bed had a study desk, meant to be shared by two boys, and at that hour, I was sitting alone at my desk, my head buried in my textbook. The absolute silence in the entire hostel allowed me to devote undivided attention to the book in front of me. I was battling with a particularly tough question that was sure to be asked in the paper when I heard a low but sharp voice.

'Jay, *kya kar raha hai* [What are you doing]?'

'Just studying,' I replied as a reflex and turned to look. Suddenly, I felt a chill in my bones. I found myself staring at the vacant wall behind me, and I saw that all the boys were already sleeping in their bunk beds. What terrified me all the more was that my gaze had fallen on the one other bed except mine that was empty, in the far corner of the room—Ashish's.

But that voice had been so clear!

I snapped out of my reverie and back into the real world. All of it came back to me in that one instant—the recent loss of Ashish and the subsequent discovery of his body—and the numbing sensation of that singular bodiless voice overlapped those memories.

That was when I realized that the voice—it freaks me out to think of it even to this day—belonged to Ashish.

What gave me some strength was the fact that I was not alone. My friends were in the dorm, even though they were asleep. I thought of waking them up, but I didn't. Instead, I walked around a bit to see if someone had played a prank, but there seemed to be no chance of that.

I was still shivering fifteen minutes later when I returned to bed, drew up the blanket over my head and slept.

I was only eleven, mind you. My condition that night was unimaginable.

———

It was small mercy that the previous night's incident stayed out of my mind till I finished my test. But the moment I stepped out of the exam hall, the memory sprang to life again. Over lunch, I thought of the voice, and the more I thought of it, with a fully conscious mind now, the more certain I was that it was Ashish's. It had the same intonation, the same hint of cheerfulness mixed with the intention to intrude and break into gossip. In fact, I had this nauseating feeling throughout the day that he might be lurking around somewhere, waiting to spring a nasty surprise on me.

That night, I planned to not be the last one to stay up. I raced through my notes and went to bed with all the others and even mumbled a little prayer before my head hit the pillow.

41

At some point during the night, my eyes opened all of a sudden. I had the sense of being in deep slumber, and that something had shaken me awake. In fact, there was a clammy feeling on my arm, as if someone had grabbed me there with a cold hand not moments ago. Soaked in sweat and fear despite the cold of the night, I raised my arm to look at it, when I felt someone's breath blowing into my ear and a clear sentence uttered directly into it:

'Jay, *uth jaa, yaar* [Wake up, buddy] . . .'

I was sleeping on the bottom bunk, and on hearing that voice, I got up so fast that I hit my head on the bar of the top bunk. I screamed out and my friends woke up. Feeling foolish, I told them I had hurt myself when standing up to go to the bathroom.

Later in bed with my eyes tightly shut, I tried to convince myself that this was only my mind playing tricks. I was also terrified that my friends would come to know of my state, and knowing how ruthless boys in hostel can be, I did not want to be the laughing stock of the dorm. My only hope was that it would pass before anyone got wind of it.

———

Over the next few days, I heard Ashish's voice increasingly often. Once, in the bathroom, when I felt a hand falling over my shoulder. At another time, I saw a movement outside the window of the dorm in the dead of the night, and a third time, the window slammed so hard that Tabish woke up to see what it was.

What consumed my thoughts was whether this was happening only to me or to others in our dorm too. After all, Ashish was friends with everyone and there was no reason why I should be a specific target. But, obviously, I could not ask anyone directly about it. What I did was mention Ashish a couple of times when the group was sitting together, but apart from a general feeling of loss and grief, they displayed no other emotion. There wasn't the remotest hint that anyone else was being haunted by his ghost, or whatever it was, in the manner that I was.

Then, one day, when I could take it no longer, I decided to speak with Tabish. He was the only one who I thought could understand my plight.

But the moment I described what was happening to me, all the colour disappeared from his face.

'What are you saying, dude?' he burst out. 'Is that why you have been acting so weird lately?'

'Weird? Do you think I am acting weird?'

'Of course! All that waking up and screaming suddenly in the middle of the night . . . that mumbling . . . I see it, Jay. Something is wrong with you. I think you should meet the counsellor tomorrow.'

I understood that I could not discuss the matter any further with Tabish. Maybe he was right. I debated in my mind whether I should really speak with the counsellor and unload my worries on her. But I did not have an option because, the next day after our test, Tabish himself dragged me to the counsellor's office.

The counsellor was a kindly lady named Winnie Bakshi. I had often seen her in the office but never thought that someday I'd be sitting in front of her myself. That morning, however, it was meant to be. Initially, I was reserved about opening up to her, but once I began recounting my experiences, I just went on. Perhaps it helped that she heard me out with a patient ear and there was a compassionate, non-judgemental expression on her face as I spoke.

After I finished telling her about everything, Ms Bakshi graced me with a warm smile. Addressing me by my name, she said, 'Jay, you are having a tough time. I can understand. You are young, and Ashish was a close friend. Moreover, he had such a personality that he left a mark on all of us. In fact, some of us adults are also finding it difficult to cope with his sudden demise. You are but a child.'

She touched my arm with comforting reassurance and went on, 'But what you are going through is quite a common occurrence that happens when someone close suddenly passes away. These are just manifestations of his memories that you still have. Somewhere, subconsciously, you miss him. That is just what this is. Don't be afraid. It's a normal coping mechanism. Ghosts don't exist, my dear child.'

I walked out of her office in a daze. Tabish was by my side, grinning like a Cheshire cat, perhaps because his point, that there was no ghost, had been proven.

Still, I could not get over it. The other unusual things I witnessed could be explained away, but that voice was definitely not a figment of my imagination. It was not merely an echo coming from my mourning mind. With all due respect to Ashish, who was a fantastic buddy of mine—and I still miss him at times—I don't think I was grieving all that much. How much can an eleven-year-old grieve anyway? Certainly not so much as to start hallucinating.

No, sir! That voice was certainly not an illusion; it was real. There really were words that had been articulated, spoken aloud, regular, proper words produced from someone's throat. And not just anyone's throat; it was Ashish's voice. Of that I am unshakeably certain to this day.

Not knowing what this spirit was after was a source of huge torment for me. That evening, I called up my father and told him that I couldn't stay in that part of the hostel any longer. Take me back home, I begged him. He tried to placate me at first. Whatever! I just wanted to get out of there. My father had heard of Ashish's death and he heard me out with concern now, but his final advice was quite practical—to stick around till the end of the exams, which was only a few more days away, and then I'd be returning home for the break anyway.

———

That night, there was great excitement in the dorm. The other boys had come to know of what was happening to me. Their questions were endless, and I answered them as much as I could, but when I could take it no more, I simply said, 'Well, if you guys don't believe me, stay up tonight. He comes at around 12.30 every night.'

There was a stunned silence in the room for a few moments. You could have literally heard the cogwheels of their brains turning at mighty speed.

'Okay, we will!' Tabish pronounced. 'Come on, guys, it will be kind of an adventure.'

Ananya chimed in, 'Yes, we will stay up. We'll turn off the lights and stay in our beds, but won't sleep. Let's see what happens.'

Truth be told, I had mixed feelings about the whole affair. There was also a twinge of sadness, for I did not know why Ashish was trying to get to me. And now I had made every boy in the dorm eager to meet him. What if Ashish's spirit got disgruntled and did something that we could not control?

Anyway, the game was set. At 11 p.m., when the lights went out, all of us ducked into our beds. We pulled up the blankets over our faces, but we didn't sleep. Now and then, someone would say something softly and keep a conversation going. That helped kill the time, and it was actually a relief to know that whatever happened, it would happen to all of us collectively.

As the minutes ticked closer to the appointed time, conversation dimmed. Apprehensions began to creep in, no doubt, and everyone's breathing became palpably heavier. Nervous shuffling sounds could be heard from all the bunk beds, and after a point, there was absolute silence.

The time had come.

The silence was so thick now that it was suffocating. Everyone stayed tucked inside their blankets, their heads covered; no one dared even peep out. Only our heavy breathing could be heard, as if what we had inside our chests wasn't a pair of lungs but a pair of bellows.

And in that absolutely crystal-clear moment of silence, I could distinctly hear—

—a shuffling of footsteps.

The sound came from the door of the dorm, as if someone was coming in. But it was impossible for anyone to enter that way, as we had locked every door and window from the inside.

I stayed absolutely still, not daring to move a muscle.

I did not even know whether any of the others could hear that sound, and for the moment, there was no way to find out.

I felt the footsteps inching closer to me. They came right up to my bed, and I broke into a sweat, still shivering within. Then I heard the footsteps moving past.

Next thing I know, I heard it—a lucid whisper, just like on those previous nights. But this time, it called out to someone else. It said:

'Tabish, *tu jaag raha hai, cheater* [You are still awake, cheater]!'

I could hear Tabish's bed creaking. He was probably trembling with fear.

The voice went on, 'Ananya, *tu bhi jaag raha hai* [You are awake too]!'

'Vijay, *chal, koi game khelte hai, yaar* [Come on, let's play a game, buddy]!'

47

'Gaurav, *kahaani sunega* [Would you like to hear a story]?'

And thus it went on. The voice, whatever it was, named each and every boy in the dorm that night. It did not name me, but as the last name was called, I could feel a slight patting on my leg as if the thing was gesturing to me that it was now leaving.

We stayed dead still in our blankets for several long minutes, and only when it was absolutely quiet again did we slowly come out, one by one.

Someone shone a flashlight throughout the dorm. Apart from the frightened faces of the seventeen of us, we could see no other around.

But then the flashlight caught something that made us gasp. It was near the door.

There was a patch of red mud near the door, an indistinct print of a pair of footsteps, and the mud itself was the kind we recognized from the forest that had now been cordoned off.

That night, we pulled our bunk beds closer and lay awake the whole night.

———

Today, almost twenty years have passed to that time. Ashish is dead and gone. That hostel night is behind us. None of us reported what had happened to the authorities as we had to leave for our break in the following two days anyway. And try as we might, there was no way to rationalize or even believe what had happened to us.

But when we resumed school, we found that the entire dorm was locked and barricaded. We were told to move to another dorm, with no specific reason given. We could only conjecture what the reason might have been. Why was a fully functional dorm locked out like that? Had someone from the authorities had an experience too? We will never know.

For the rest of my term in the school, which I continued to attend till I passed out of class nine, Ashish never appeared again.

I happened to bump into Ananya five years ago. He spoke to me about the episode and informed me that he had recently visited the school and the dorm was still locked. He had walked through the halls and even found the same rusty lock the authorities had put in all those years ago. A caretaker who recognized him told him that the dorm had never been opened since that time.

Strange are the things that befall us, and those that happen without motive or provocation are the strangest. Try as I might, I haven't been able to hit upon a satisfying answer as to why I was the only one to hear Ashish's voice for the longest time. Why had Ashish's spirit lingered like that? Had he simply wanted to bid us a final goodbye? I have tried to rationalize these things, but all I can come up with are theories.

Possibly, it was after this time that I began to develop the faculties of an empath—one who is described in the paranormal world as a person with a heightened sixth sense, one who is able to feel emotions in others and perceive things in the surroundings that most people cannot. These are the things that we variously term 'paranormal' or 'supernatural'. Maybe there was a tiny bit of these qualities in me back then, which made me perceive Ashish before the other boys in the hostel did.

Over time, this sense in me has sharpened, so much so that I now rely on it more than I do on my paranormal devices and gadgets.

I have another view too. I used to think that my abilities have been heightened given my line of work, but whenever I think of the Darjeeling hostel incident, in hindsight, I think differently. Maybe it was the other way round. Maybe I was always an empath and that is why Ashish chose to reveal himself to me first, and I was the channel through which he appeared to the other boys later. I have, sometimes, felt that I am a conduit for these spirits, though, so far, I have not had a direct experience of being used that way.

I also get this strong feeling that this was the turning point that put me on the path of paranormal investigation. I will be honest and admit that whenever I am conducting these investigations, a part of my mind floats back to those nights at the hostel. I have never mentioned it to anyone before, but through all my work in the realm of the paranormal, I hope to someday understand what Ashish was really trying to convey to me.

Who knows, maybe one day I will go to the hostel again and conduct an investigation. But that place belongs to my childhood; it sparks nostalgia for me. Going there again will certainly not be an easy thing to do; it will demand every ounce of my courage.

What keeps the flame burning is this one thought—maybe somewhere in the darkness of that dorm room that has been barricaded for two decades, Ashish's spirit is still there, his arms reaching out, a radiant smile on his face, waiting for someone to come and hear his story.

3

The Salt Witch of the
Lambi Dehar Mines

THERE ARE MANY tales about the Lambi Dehar mines of Uttarakhand, almost as many as the number of mouths that narrate them. When I went to these mines in 2015, without really realizing what a nightmare I was getting into, I had a chance to see for myself why the locals avoided this place like a curse. Even in terms of sheer geographical magnitude, this is not some nondescript haunted hamlet. Locals speak of an incident that occurred in 1996 when a jaw-dropping number of workers—20,000—got mysteriously trapped in these mines and eventually died.

Even today, on silent nights like the one when I visited this place, you can hear the wails of these anguished souls struggling to get out.

Follow me into this top haunted site in Uttarakhand as I delve into the myth of the 'Salt Witch' who laid a curse on this place, and tell you all about how I came very close to my own death.

In January 2015, when I was working with a media company in South Extension, New Delhi, I received a call that would lead me to one of the most hellish experiences of my life. The call had come all the way from Dehradun, and the caller was a real estate broker named Dipanshu. He got right down to business without any preamble. Very succinctly, he told me that he knew of me through my videos on the Internet and wondered if I'd be interested in investigating something for him.

He told me the details. His firm had been trying to sell a plot of land on the outskirts of Mussoorie. As he described it, the land had everything going for it—a pristine location in the Himalayan foothills, a desirable destination for a vacation home and a low asking price—and yet the firm was unable to dispose of it.

I was still trying to figure out how I fit in, when he fumbled, 'The locals believe there's something wrong with the property.'

'Something wrong? As in?' I asked.

'Well . . .' There was a pause where I could almost hear his thoughts whirring. 'People say there's some negative energy around the place.'

Bingo!

'I know of your reputation as a paranormal investigator, sir!' he told me. 'I have watched all your videos. Could you please make a trip to Mussoorie with me so you can look at this place and tell me if there is something wrong with it? Help us get to the bottom of the mystery, if there is any? Money is not an issue. Could you, please?'

His tone was insistent. But more than the persuasion, I could sense something else. It was fear. Oh yes, I could smell the fear right away.

'What if there's really something there?' I asked.

'If there is, there is,' he said. 'But if there isn't, your visit will put some rumours to rest. Maybe it'll help us to sell the plot.'

The proposal sounded intriguing, and in any case, I thrive on such visits. I took a day to think it over and find out more about the place. The following day, Dipanshu called me punctually at the time I had instructed him to, and I gave him my go-ahead.

I could hear the excitement in his voice after I conveyed my consent. But little did either of us know what we were getting into.

———

I reached Mussoorie on 9 February 2015, after wrapping up some of my ongoing projects. As my bus drove me from Delhi to Dehradun, I could not escape the feeling of ascending to a higher plane of existence, which is normal when one is moving closer to the Himalayas. There is something about this gigantic mountain range that you just cannot escape. Even from hundreds of miles away, you can feel the pull. And this time, I was visiting with such a bold purpose that it put quite a sinister spin on things.

Dipanshu was waiting with his bike at the Dehradun bus stand to pick me up. In the flesh, he was quite the antithesis of the man I had spoken to on the phone. Hearing his guttural baritone, I had expected an older, burly man, possibly with a beard and pondering eyes. The man I met instead was of average height, clean-shaven and quite young. He was dressed in a shirt and trousers, the attire of an office-going employee. When he spotted me, he came running up to me and insisted on taking my bag.

'Jay sir! How was the journey?' he asked.

'Please call me Jay,' I insisted. 'The trip was good. I am glad I started out early in the morning. My lungs are filled with fresh mountain air now.'

He laughed. 'There'll be more of that for the next two days. I have booked a lodge for you. Calm and peaceful place. It's off-season, so no tourists either. And please do not eat the hotel food. I will bring food for you. My wife's a wonderful cook.'

His hospitality endeared him to me. I hopped on his bike and in a minute we were snaking through the meandering uphill roads that would take us to the lodge.

On the way, he told me about the plot. He talked quite technically about it, using figures and measurements that did not interest me much. He said that the place was completely new; no one had lived there before or used it for anything else.

That night, he came to the lodge bringing home-cooked food just as he had promised. The steaming hot aroma hit my nostrils even before he opened the tiffin. There was simple dal with chapattis, rice and vegetables, but for a person like me who lives away from home for such long periods of time, anything homemade is a veritable feast. I did not speak a word until I had wolfed down a few bites.

Then I asked him, 'So, Dipanshu, what do you think of the stories about the place? The negative energy you told me about, I mean . . .'

Dipanshu was sitting beside me. He stopped chewing mid-morsel when I asked that question. He swallowed hard and then said, 'To be honest, I think they are all just old wives' tales, nothing else.'

'Really?'

'Jay, once you know the villagers better, you will understand. Here in the mountains, there isn't much entertainment. People find their own ways to amuse themselves. To add to that, almost everyone here is a fantastic storyteller.'

'So you think people are just fabricating things?'

'I won't comment on that,' he said. 'At any rate, you are here now. You will find out for yourself.'

With that, he clammed up. I did not probe any further either. I understood that he had a bias here. He needed to sell the property. It was definitely not in his best interests to fan the fire around any ghostly tales about the place.

———

That night, before falling asleep to the rhythm of crickets and cicadas in the valley below, I made up my mind to approach this place with no preconceived notions. Hearsay would not help. I had to take this up with an open mind and be ready to accept what I was going to see and experience.

I woke up two hours earlier than the slated hour when Dipanshu was to arrive to pick me up. I had to equip myself. Into my trustworthy backpack I stuffed my many flashlights, an infrared thermometer, a K2 meter and a new addition—a PSB-11 Spirit Box. I had acquired this device only recently and, to be honest, I was itching to put it to use. The PSB-11 works more or less like a radio that captures bandwidths. But while radios can only catch frequencies within a particular range, this device can tune in even to frequencies that are beyond the human audible range.

The path leading to Mussoorie was just as I had imagined—a narrow route snaking between hills on one side and a deep valley on the other. It had several blind turns where trucks and buses suddenly emerged like monsters on some vindictive mission. Now, while the paranormal does not unnerve me much, it is such contrivances that disorient me. The chances of someone plummeting to their death in a fraction of a second by slipping down these valleys or being hit by a truck driven by a sleepy drunkard are much higher than being haunted to death by some unseen spirit.

We were riding mostly uphill. With Dipanshu focusing on the road, I had a good opportunity to survey the surroundings. We were almost at the top when I noticed something incongruous about one of the distant hills. It was around 15 kilometres away from where we were riding and there appeared to be some kind of tumbledown structure hanging from the hill. For some reason, my senses were heightened.

'Dipanshu, what is that?' I asked, pointing.

Dipanshu did not turn to look but he understood what I was asking about. 'Those are the Lambi Dehar mines,' he said. 'Also known as the Lambidhar mines.'

'Mines? You have mines here?'

He nodded. 'Limestone used to be mined here. In fact, a lot of limestone came from these parts in those days.'

'*Used to be*? What do you mean?'

'The mines are shut down now,' he said simply. 'It was a court order. A Supreme Court order actually. Too much risk. I don't know much but there was some accident here twenty years ago. Many people died. After that they shut down the mines.'

'Oh!'

As we rode along, I kept looking back at the outline of the mines receding in the distance, now appearing like a yawning slit in the mountainside. It was strange how they looked like some kind of touristy marvel and at the same time like a death trap for anyone who dared to venture inside.

Ten minutes later, Dipanshu parked his bike on the side of the road.

'Here we are!' he announced.

I got off and took a look around. The road was quite narrow, flanked by stretches of land on either side, both equally barren and desolate. The confusion must have been apparent on my face because Dipanshu took me by the hand to one of them and made me stand at a particular spot.

'This is the plot,' he said. 'It is two acres.'

That was all there was, actually. The plot was as unremarkable as it could be. Just flat land layered with pebbles, nothing more. Nothing constructed on it. There was not even the usual signboard that warned off trespassers. At one edge of the rectangular plot, a herd of goats grazed idly at the sparse shrubbery that dotted the barren land and bleated with contentment.

Wordlessly, I walked along the plot. There were some stone markings serving as a boundary, and I walked along that line. I circled it once entirely and then came back to the centre. Dipanshu stood patiently with his hands thrust into the pockets of his trousers.

My backpack was still on my shoulders. I didn't feel the need to open it.

During my investigations, I always rely on my initial instincts first. Whenever I visit a place for the first time, I take a moment to feel its vibe. Places, like people, give off vibes. Not all of us can sense these all the time, but, on occasion, I have. It happens with all of us to an extent. Sometimes you enter someone's apartment for the first time and everything is spick and span and homely, but you still feel that something is off. This is what we call a negative vibe. When something bad prevails in a place, there is a certain energy it exudes. Perhaps years of dealing with such energy zones has created a certain innate radar in me.

Here, though, the fact was that I did not feel any negative vibes at all as I walked around the plot.

Nothing seemed to be amiss. Dipanshu looked at me expectantly, and I did not know what he was really hoping to hear, but I didn't have anything to tell him right way.

As I stood there thinking of the right words to say, I happened to look over Dipanshu's shoulder. There they were, the Lambi Dehar mines, now a spot in the distance but appearing to be cleanly placed on his shoulder, as though he were lifting the burden of it.

I could not really be sure from where we stood, but from what I could discern, it seemed as though the entrance to the mines directly overlooked the plot.

'Dipanshu, I don't think anything is wrong with this particular place,' I began tentatively.

'What do you mean? Then why do people say—'

I cut him short. 'But I do think there's some influence.'

He looked at me unblinkingly.

'Look there, Dipanshu.' I physically turned him around and indicated the mines. 'I think your problems stem from there.'

'The mines?'

I nodded. 'What do you say to a trip there right now?'

———

Our destination was 4 kilometres away from the plot, but the distance seemed longer, owing to the zigzag, winding road. Dipanshu was still not sure why we were going to the mines instead of investigating his plot, but out of courtesy, I suppose, he didn't say anything.

I asked him, 'What was the accident about?'

I hadn't given much thought to it before. Accidents are not abnormal in mines. But the intriguing thing in this case was how those mines came to be built there on the top of the hill in the first place. The entire topography of the land was prone to landslides. Why would anyone do any mining there at all?

'I am not too sure,' said Dipanshu. 'There are too many stories. Seems like the miners were trapped due to a landslide and suffocated to death.'

'That bad? How many casualties?'

This was where I got my first true shock during the trip. The number that he offered in reply, so coolly at that, shook me from within.

'Around twenty thousand.'

'Twenty thousand!' I shouted. Hearing my raised voice, a driver going in the opposite direction gave me a stern look. 'Stop the bike! Stop it right now!'

Dipanshu applied the brakes. 'What happened?'

I needed a moment to process this new information. I got off the bike, walked to the edge of the road, looked at the valley below and took a deep breath. Then I returned to him and said, 'You tell me twenty thousand people died in those mines?'

'That's what people say, yes.'

'Oh, my dear Dipanshu, I need to confirm this. Is there anyone who will know for sure?'

Dipanshu was now staring at me as if he were suspicious of my mental stability. After a moment's pause, he said, 'There's an old chai–biscuit shop just near the mines. The old man there will know more than I do.'

'Well, let's go see this old man then.'

61

With my mind in a whirl and my bones already rattling at the thought of so many disgruntled spirits, we resumed our journey.

———

The old scrawny man at that little establishment was no less than a wonder. Who were his customers at that remote height anyway, so far removed from habitable civilization? When we parked next to him, he looked at us in puzzlement, almost as if he did not want us there. We ordered our teas and I swung into conversation.

'Kaka [Uncle], do you get many customers?'

He looked at me with a world-weariness that was almost painful to watch and replied, 'I get my share. This road connects Hathipaon with Mussoorie. I get the stray traveller who uses this road.'

'Kaka, I am Jay. I have come all the way from Delhi. My friend here has a plot of land which he is not able to sell.'

The man guffawed. 'How will it sell?' he said between snorts. 'You see those ruins behind me? Those are the Lambi Dehar mines. Haven't you heard of the salt witch of the mines?'

A low whistle escaped my lips.

'Salt witch? Tell me more, kaka.'

Kaka evidently had time on his hands. He had no customers waiting at that time. His head tilted to one side, he had a faraway look in his eyes. And he narrated a story, by the end of which it felt as if my legs were about to give way.

'This story goes back more than a hundred years, when the British still used to rule India,' he began. 'At that time, Mussoorie was a small, unknown town. One year, a British officer fell in love with the pleasant climate of the place and made his home here. He lived somewhere on the hills that way. During one of his walks, he landed on this spot here. At that time, there was nothing to see. But when he looked closely, he saw a small hut right on top of the hill. He asked the locals and found out that only an old woman stayed in the hut. The locals believed the woman was eccentric and steered clear from her.

'After a few days, curiosity got the best of the Englishman. Unable to restrain himself, the *firangi* trekked up the hill and came to the hut. The woman was there, hunched over her *chulha*, preparing food for herself and humming a local song. The woman saw the tall officer standing at the door of the hut and welcomed him in. She offered him tea. The officer asked her why she lived alone. She told him in a strange dialect of Hindi that she was a nomad and this was the way her people lived.

'When the British officer returned home and took off his shoes, he was surprised to find some white powder on the soles. There was quite a bit of it; his shoes were caked in it. That powder was limestone of the best quality. Putting two and two together, he concluded that the entire hill had a reserve of high-quality limestone within.

'That was what changed the entire course of events. Almost overnight, the officer ordered mines to be built all over the place. Within a week, a posse of construction workers arrived at the old woman's hut and pulled it down. The woman witnessed the devastation with pained eyes but she went away without a word of complaint. No one has seen her since.

'In time, the mines became a hub of activity in the town. People from nearby villages came here to seek employment. Old folk like me know how much these mines did to improve the reputation of Mussoorie.'

We listened in silence. Mid-way through the story, our teas had gone cold. The old man generously filled fresh glasses of tea for us.

I took a sip and realized how much I needed it to warm the chill within. I asked him, 'What about the accident, kaka?'

Before he continued, the old man looked back at the entrance to the mines, as if asking permission to spill this sordid part of the tale.

'So you have heard of the accident? Well, who hasn't? When the British left India, the mines were shut down for a while. They opened again a few years later and continued to function for several decades, until 1996 to be precise, which is when the accident took place.

'I wasn't here at the time of the accident. But I have heard tales. On that particular day, there were tens of thousands of people working in there. Workers, miners, supervisors, all. Men braving great risks and hauling up tons of limestone. It was business as usual. That morning, a woman appeared at the gates. She had a child with her and carried a tiffin, which she said was for her husband. It was routine for the miners' wives

64

to bring food for their husbands, and so the gatekeeper let her in. She left her child outside and entered the mines. No one saw her after that.

'Now the abnormal thing about this visit was that the child apparently just vanished right in front of the gatekeeper's eyes. The man was sitting outside watching the child play. He let his gaze wander for a second and when he looked back, the child was gone. He mentioned this to a few people, but no one paid any heed.

'That night, work was on in full swing in the mines. In the middle of the night, the supervisors who lived in huts outside heard a loud crashing sound. They came out running and saw that the entryway to the mines had collapsed. Everyone was trapped inside, for that was the only way in and out of the mines. The supervisors could hear the men inside screaming about some green toxic gas that was making their skins peel off, right up to the bone, but they could do nothing.

'By morning, the cries had died down. The authorities were called. The mines were blasted open. And what followed was the most macabre sight this place has ever seen. There were bodies heaped upon bodies, all torn and burnt away, all dead. It is said that fifty thousand miners died in those mines that night.'

'Fifty thousand! I heard twenty . . .' I said.

'Fifty, twenty, what does it matter? Have you ever heard of a tragedy of such catastrophic proportions?'

I shook my head.

'The woman with the child was a *chudail*,' the old man said, his face now very close to mine, and I could see a glint in his eyes. 'She is a special kind of witch, this one, a solitary witch. They live alone and do not like to be disturbed. If anyone disturbs them, they get violent and vengeful.' Then the man looked at Dipanshu who had been silent all along. 'Brother, this is the witch that's plaguing your plot of land too. If you trust me, forget your land. Nothing good is going to come out of it anyway.'

———

One thing that the old man had said stayed with me—*solitary witch*. I had come across this in my research earlier. Different kinds of witches are mentioned in old texts, of which solitary witches are described as the most dangerous ones, who can change shape, form and age. Perhaps that was why she was able to appear as a young woman with a child. These witches are essentially ageless. Who knows for how many centuries she had been living in those mountains before the British officer found her? And who knows how many more centuries she will remain on this plane—if she really exists?

The only way to find any answers to these questions would be to enter the Lambi Dehar mines. We were already at the gate, but I was thinking twice about it now as my only companion was Dipanshu and I could distinctly hear his teeth chattering. There was no way I could take him inside with me in that condition.

I turned to him. 'Dipanshu, what do you say? I will have to explore the mines. But I think you should turn back. I can find my way back on my own.'

I thought Dipanshu would seize that opportunity and run away from the place, but what he said took me by surprise.

'No, brother,' he said, his words belying the slight aberration in his tone. 'I will come with you. I have led you here and it is only fair that I accompany you.'

'You don't understand, Dipanshu,' I said. 'I have experience with such places. You don't. Also, things could get complicated if you cannot control your feelings.'

'What do you mean?'

'Spirits feed on fear,' I explained. 'If you become afraid, it could have disastrous consequences for you.'

'Like . . . they could possess me?'

I did not want to spell it out. 'It's a possibility, yes.'

He pondered on that for a moment and shook his head firmly. 'Still, I insist. I shall go inside with you.'

The time was 6.30 now. The sun was just a slice wedged over the horizon, ready to go away for the day. Seeing that Dipanshu was quite determined about coming along with me, I stepped into the entryway. He followed.

'I am surprised that these mines are so easily accessible,' I remarked. 'I mean . . . given that great tragedy, they should have been cordoned off or something.'

Dipanshu shrugged. 'Yes, but you know . . . the authorities haven't taken this seriously. In fact, people here enter freely in the daytime. Youngsters come here for the adventure of being in a haunted location. Take selfies and whatnot. And that's not all. Walk around a bit and you will see booze bottles. Maybe even condoms.'

'That's terrible. It's disrespecting all those helpless workers who died here.'

'Sorry, brother, but that's the reality of it.'

Right at the entrance was some sort of large compound built on the mountainside. It was flat and covered with overgrown grass. On one edge of this compound was a series of stone structures, worn down over time, all of them roofless.

'It seems to be a hallmark of haunted places,' I said aloud. 'Roofless structures.'

The evening insects had begun to buzz. Now and then, you could see a firefly glowing in the fast-receding light. Suddenly, we spotted a signboard which indicated that the place where we were standing had once been the administrative block, the uppermost level of the mines.

It was time to bring out the flashlights. I took one and gave Dipanshu another. Despite his persistence, his breath was running cold now. I tapped him on the shoulder, gesturing for him to come along. And then he screamed.

It was a short sharp scream that instantly made me turn around to look at him.

His foot was poised in mid-air. There was something on the ground that he had been about to step on but had stopped just in time.

'What is it?' he asked me, not daring to look down.

I shone the light on the thing. It was black and mangled, and when I peered closer, I almost toppled over backwards.

They were two dead crows. Stinking. Their necks had been viciously twisted and broken, probably by some larger bird. Blood was still flowing out of their wounds, which indicated the deaths were recent.

'They are just crows,' I said. 'Poor dead crows.'

Dipanshu finally placed his foot on the ground.

Leaving him there, I proceeded to check the other areas of the block. Darkness sets in pretty quickly in these mountain regions. Actually, it's a mistake to enter a new haunted place once it's dark, something that I would never advise any paranormal enthusiast. The ideal way to go about it would be to do a recce in daylight, set up the equipment and then return at night to investigate.

But I had flouted my own rules and now there was no turning back. We scanned the area with the full moon's brilliance aiding our search. I walked to the very edge and came up to the huge gaping hole that was the entry to the mines. That was where I made up my mind.

I have spoken of places giving off vibes earlier. I hadn't felt any on Dipanshu's plot, but here, at the mouth of the mines, each and every nerve in my body began to tingle. I felt a creeping sensation along my scalp as I broke out in a cold sweat. It was as if something was draining out of me. Fear has a way of eliciting physical signs in you, and these were exactly those kinds of signs. I do not feel afraid as a rule, but I am not ashamed to admit, on that full moon night, as I stood facing the Lambi Dehar mines, I felt a kind of fear that I had never experienced before.

'What is it?' Dipanshu breathed into my ear.

'There is something in there. Something evil. I can sense it.' I looked at my watch. 'But it is too early to go inside. Spirits are beings of the night. Will have to wait till the night gets really dark.'

Dipanshu did not say anything. We walked back to the gate, planning to wait it out there. As we retraced the path we had covered when entering, there came a moment when our nerves were numbed to the core.

While passing the spot where Dipanshu had almost stepped on the dead crows, we had a severe fright. We saw the carcasses move. I quickly trained my flashlight on the spot, but before I could focus, we saw the crows springing back to life and, lo, right in front of our unbelieving eyes, they took flight, soaring up into the sky! Left behind now was an ugly smear of blood tracing a smudged outline of the spot on the ground.

'Those dead crows!' yelled Dipanshu. 'They . . . they just flew away!'

I was on my guard now. Despite what I planned to tell Dipanshu, more to calm his nerves than anything else, I knew this was a sign out of the ordinary. They were definitely dead carcasses, but I held back from showing my excitement at the promise of a paranormal investigation.

'Dipanshu,' I began carefully. 'Maybe they weren't dead. Maybe they were just wounded.'

'But how . . . their necks . . . '

'Happens. A predator might have gotten hold of them and they might have escaped. Crows are resilient creatures. Come on, we have a lot of ground to cover.'

Still shaking his head in disbelief, Dipanshu followed me. He could not see my face or he would have seen the glow of anticipation writ large on it.

———

We whiled away time, talking of casual things such as movies and cricket to lighten the mood. But our talks were restrained, for there was this undercurrent of sheer terror tainting our mood as we geared up to explore. At 11 p.m., it was pitch black. Even the full moon was obscured by clouds, and save the dim dots of light marking the houses in the distance, there was nothing to show that we were in the lap of civilization. With a heavy sigh, I got up and Dipanshu followed suit.

Hardly any words were exchanged between us now. I strapped on my headlight and picked up the devices. I handed Dipanshu a flashlight as we made our way to the mouth of the mines.

The moment we descended, the dank claustrophobic atmosphere began to affect us.

Inside a mine, it is akin to being locked up in a very narrow space without any opening for light or air. These places are mostly long, winding tunnels cut into the earth. As you walk along them, you cannot shake off this creepy feeling that you are entering the bowels of the earth. In some places, it gets so narrow that only one person can pass through, sideways. If that isn't the worst nightmare of a claustrophobe, I don't know what is.

And, to make matters worse, there was the constant thought of the disaster that had struck here not many years ago.

The walls had been silent witnesses to the dying screams of the thousands of workers who must have banged their fists pitifully on these very surfaces, struggling to get away, man pushing man, with not enough space for even a stampede. They must have been packed so closely together. Their violent last gasps of breath, all their desires and attachments dying away in those panic-stricken final moments, knowing that everything they had lived for was now plunging into nothingness—just thinking about it brought on a wave of nausea in me.

The negative energy this place gave out could make the blood stop in your veins.

Soon, we came to a clearing in the maze of tunnels. It was a round room-like structure with some stones piled up in the centre. It seemed like a place where the workers might have taken their breaks amid the long work hours. Dipanshu went up ahead and sat on one of the stones. I could see him breathing hard, and with a start realized that I was breathing hard too. We might be at a significant number of feet underground, for it was getting apparent that oxygen was scarce.

For the next fifteen minutes, we simply sat. Then something happened that gave me a jolt. The lights on the K2 meter suddenly went crazy. As Dipanshu and I looked on, all five lights began to blink rapidly, right up to the red zone, which is for extremely high frequencies.

This constituted the rarest of rare occurrences. Any professional in my field would probably experience this only a couple of times in their entire life. And here it was happening to me in these claustrophobic mines.

This could mean only one thing—there was definitely something here that was causing a strong electrical field to take hold.

I could not take my eyes off the meter. The fluctuation I was witnessing—it was just impossible.

I heard Dipanshu's feeble voice—'Jay . . .'

He was staring at me, his face had gone all white. 'What is that?'

He raised a spindly finger, pointing at something, staring into the distance behind me. 'There's something behind you, Jay!' he finally said, in a voice that churned my insides.

I will admit that I was afraid. Very, very afraid. This was a totally new kind of fear for me. What was it behind me that struck such terror into Dipanshu? The way he was looking at it, I thought that my last moment on earth had arrived.

I sat still. I did not turn around. The thing that was behind me, if there was indeed something, hadn't attacked me yet, but it might if I looked at it directly. And there was another reason not to look. Dipanshu's face. It was the picture of abject horror. My biggest priority right now was to take him away from this place. He could have collapsed, or even died of shock on the spot.

'Dipanshu, do as I tell you,' I told him in a low voice, but quite firmly.

'Wha-at?'

'Just stand up and leave.'

'What?'

'Go away now. Get up and use the exit on the other end and leave this place. *Right now.*'

Dipanshu locked eyes with me again. Calmed. Or at least I thought so. He did not get up.

Meanwhile, in the K2 meter, the fluctuations had stopped. The needle was back in the normal field position.

'Is that thing still behind me?' I asked him.

'N-no . . .'

'Good. Now listen. I am going still deeper into these mines. But I am not taking you with me. Get out of these mines and wait for me at the entrance.'

This time, he stood up.

Later, I asked him about what he had seen behind me, but he could not explain it properly. All he said was that it was a large hazy figure, much like a crow with giant wings tucked into its sides. But even he wasn't sure then that it wasn't an illusion.

I knew it was not. I had seen the manic dance of lights on the K2 meter.

———

After Dipanshu left, I continued to sit there for a while. I needed the spirits to know that I wasn't out to disturb them. Staying passive was a way of giving that signal. One of the things I have learnt is that all paranormal entities feed off a frightened and excited state of mind. If you show more activity, they turn more malevolent. That is one reason why paranormal entities do not harm you when you are asleep, even though they might be present in the same room with you all the time.

It was 2.30 a.m. when I stood up next. I had a drink of water, took a deep breath and then shone my light into the tunnel that went deeper into the earth.

This was terror to the extreme. Being in that place surrounded by the shadows of death, with no hope of coming out alive, was by far the most hair-raising experience of my life. I could have turned back and left. I had achieved my objective of proving to Dipanshu that there was something vile about this place. But now I found myself thinking beyond that. My inherent curiosity about the world beyond the normal had gripped me. Something told me that whatever I found in that space down there would be nothing like any human has ever known before.

That single-minded incentive sucked me in. That is the kind of thrill that drives me. Some people jump off cliffs, some race cars at death-defying speeds. I challenge haunted spaces.

I was inside the deepest section of the mines now, walking along the narrow path that the miners might have trod on while they had been still breathing. I made my way ahead, step by step, scrutinizing every inch of the place. There was only the sound of my footsteps and my heaving and breathing, and then—

—there was another sound.

I froze in my tracks. The other sound stopped too.

I took another step. And I heard it again.

I moved ahead, taking smaller steps now, and there it was, growing clearer now . . . closer . . .

. . . the sound of someone . . . or *something* following me.

It was quite distinct—the sound of steps treading on the pebbles and displacing them with each step.

This time, I turned around. It was an abrupt and deliberate movement, designed to glimpse whatever it was that was following me, even if it attempted to hide.

But the thing that was following me had no intention of hiding. Even as I turned to look at it right in the eye, that thing stood its ground, grinning at me.

What I saw following me was a wolflike creature.

This one looked like a wolf in all respects, and perhaps it was just that, a wolf that had strayed into the depths of these mines, but I knew by pure instinct that this was no ordinary animal. For starters, it was much taller than a wolf. And its eyes bore that red glint of malice that predators have when they are poised to attack.

I had to be brave. There was no scope for fear any more.

If it were indeed a wolf, I wouldn't want my epitaph to read—*Jay Alani. Paranormal Investigator. Killed by a Wolf.*

In our training for such investigations, we are also taught how to deal with natural threats such as predators. With no other apparent option at my disposal, I decided to test my survival tricks and shone all my flashlights, full force, right into the eyes of the creature.

Now, a real wolf would have bolted away on account of the cumulative glare of all those lights. Wolves are nocturnal creatures that cannot bear bright lights. But that's not what happened. I flashed the lights at once, and was myself blinded for an instant. When I regained clear vision, I had the very faint impression that the creature was still there, staring at me with its sad but menacing eyes. For the second time that night, I had the feeling that I had strayed too far, that I was done for. But when I blinked and then opened my eyes, the thing was gone.

It took me several minutes to compose myself. That creature was definitely not a wolf. Whatever it was, it was not a wolf. My heart threatening to explode in my chest, I stared at the end of the tunnel for any sign that it might return.

Thankfully, it didn't.

———

I had reached the farthest end of the mines by now, or so it appeared to me. Bracing myself for things to get infinitely worse, I stood there for a while, surveying the place and trying to breathe normally. Then I brought out the big bad boy—my PSB-11 Spirit Box.

Forgetting all inhibitions for a moment, I began tuning it up excitedly, the way a little boy would play fascinatedly with a new toy. It must have been quite a sight—me standing there in the middle of that clear space, pointing the box in every direction of the tunnel, trying to perceive whatever I could.

There was a babble of sounds, which delighted me more than it scared me. Such sounds are often present in the space around us, but our human ears cannot discern them. My device was expected to pick up precisely such auditory signals, proving its high sensitivity.

I strained to listen more closely to the garbled sounds. I shut my eyes to focus, and out of the blue—I was not sure then, but I am now—I heard a female voice.

The voice had spoken a single word, quite clearly, in Hindi. It stood out distinctly against all the noise.

'*Jao!*'

Go away!

That was it. Go away. The thing that wanted me out had made its presence felt. I felt my bones begin to shake.

At any moment, I realized, that thing could manifest before me. And if that rasping, grating voice was any indication, I was sure that it belonged to the solitary witch, the salt witch of the Lambi Dehar mines, around whom such legends were woven.

But why was I afraid? Wasn't this what I had come for?

I told myself that a hundred times in that one minute, and I continued standing like that, not allowing my fear to reveal itself physically in any form. In any such battle, the key is to stand your ground. Even spirits think twice before harming brave-hearts.

I stood thus and spoke boldly in Hindi, 'I will go away from here now, but I refuse to be afraid of you. Whatever you are, don't try to do anything to scare me, for I won't be afraid. Come and confront me in your most terrifying form if you wish. Kill me if you wish. But I mean you no harm, and I want you to know that.'

With those words, I retraced my steps and left.

I turned off all devices. They were done serving their purpose anyway. I stuffed everything in my backpack as I walked, and with only one flashlight on, I proceeded towards the exit.

And I need to tell you this. All along the path that I traversed to the exit of the mines, I could feel something walking behind me. This time, I was sure it wasn't the wolf-like creature. Relying on my restricted peripheral vision, I could make out that the thing following me was large, like a shadow that looms right up to the ceiling, and it was just as broad. All through that walk back, though I did not show it on the outside in any way, I was praying that this being would not consider me harmful and harm me in return. Each step I took felt heavy like lead, but I suppressed the urge to look back.

It is the turning back to look that usually proves fatal.

———

It was 4.30 in the morning when I emerged, unharmed. Dipanshu was sitting on the ground, propped up against his bike, dozing. I woke him up and told him that we had to leave the place as soon as we could. Overjoyed to hear that, he got on the bike and I followed.

The following morning, when he came to meet me one last time, I told him gravely, 'Dipanshu, brother, one thing is for sure. You have to forget about this plot. The presence out here is too ominous for any kind of habitation. You must not put anyone else's life at risk.'

He agreed to convey the message to his company, and with that assurance, I returned to Delhi.

There are many legends about the Lambi Dehar mines, and each of them puts a new spin on things. Maybe those unexplained road accidents in the vicinity are also a part of the witch's curse. Not many can explain these things, at least not as lucidly as I have done here, but one thing is for sure— the salt witch of the Lambi Dehar mines is still very much there inside, alive, waiting for her next gullible victim.

4

The Forbidden Fort of Bhangarh

BHANGARH FORT, SITUATED in Alwar district, Rajasthan, is officially the most 'haunted' site in India. The place bears a notice put up by the Archaeological Survey of India, forbidding people to stay here from 6 p.m. to 6 a.m. Despite the ominous warning, this seventeenth-century monument sees a lot of tourist activity.

Over the centuries, several incidents that have been reported to have occurred in and around the fort can be attributed to paranormal forces. Local villagers are terrified to even talk about the fort, which, according to legend, was destroyed by an evil black magician 400 years ago and has since then become the abode of trapped, vengeful spirits. By many first-hand accounts, the curse persists to this day.

Bhangarh had been on my list for a long time, and I got a chance to visit it in 2015. Here, I describe my experiences at the fort, which include some unbelievable findings that I had hitherto kept to myself.

During the dusty summer of 2015, I was in the capital city of New Delhi, braving the heat and everything that comes with it, working at an office job. It was in the middle of this hectic and torturous schedule that I had a brush with India's officially most haunted location—Bhangarh Fort.

The opportunity presented itself in the middle of May, when our office announced a leave period of seven days. None of us were expecting this windfall from our strict management. Frenzied plans were made on how to spend the unanticipated holidays, only to be dissed just as soon. Some of us colleagues decided to spend the week at a Himalayan hill station, but as is wont with most plans you make with friends, this one too fell apart even before it could come through. Everyone dropped out, and suddenly I was looking at seven spare days looming in front of me with absolutely nothing to do.

Twiddling my thumbs purposelessly is misery to me. It is just not in my DNA to put my feet up and sit idly without any objective to drive me. After just two days of inaction, I realized that the only way to stay sane would be to go somewhere to keep myself occupied. And the thought of Bhangarh strongly presented itself to me.

I had heard of Bhangarh in a casual conversation a few years ago. A friend had described how two of his cousins had dared to visit the haunted city twenty years ago, and had never returned. There had been an elaborate manhunt for their bodies, but not a trace was found. When I conducted further inquiries about the place, I heard that dozens of people had gone missing in Bhangarh over the last few years. Even the local officials had drawn a blank in these cases. When someone is reported missing in Bhangarh, the case files are closed as soon as they are opened, I was told.

Bhangarh Fort is located in a small village surrounded by nothing but desert land for several kilometres all around. One would not be able to just vanish from the area. There is surely a deep hidden mystery in there that no one has dared to unearth. Or, more likely, those who have tried haven't lived to tell the tale.

I took out my laptop and did some more research. That part wasn't difficult at all. No sooner did I enter the word 'Bhangarh' in the search bar than I was bombarded with tens of thousands of results. There were stories of people who never came back (hundreds of missing persons!), articles on how even the local villagers never loiter in these premises after sunset, accounts of strange disembodied sounds that would unnerve even the most stout-hearted and sudden chills and winds that seemed to come from the ramparts of the fort and sweep over the landscape. Every horror trope that we have ever come across, I found it linked to Bhangarh in some Internet article or the other, making it seem like a veritable hub of paranormal activity.

Naturally, my curiosity was piqued. All of a sudden, I felt that my vacation would now find some meaning. I'd utilize it to do the one thing I had wished to do for so long, which had eluded me though, somehow or the other—to investigate the deep dark secret of the haunted Bhangarh Fort of Rajasthan.

The following morning itself, I hired a cab from Delhi to Bhangarh, a distance of approximately 235 kilometres. The dusty journey took most of the day, and it was sundown by the time I reached a village called Dausa, which is about 30 kilometres away from Bhangarh Fort; the locals told me that this was the only place I would be able to find any semblance of accommodation and food for miles around. Heeding their advice, I decided to stop for the night at Dausa and checked into a hotel.

At the hotel, I stated my purpose of visit to the manager, a staunch Rajasthani man with a shining tilak on his forehead. The moment I mentioned the fort, his shifty eyes stilled. Haltingly, he asked me about it, and when I said that I planned to spend the next day and night at Bhangarh, his face momentarily paled. I had the feeling that he wanted to tell me something, perhaps dissuade me, but he shrugged and walked away as if he had decided that it was not his job to warn me.

The following morning at seven, when the summer sun had already started its business of singeing the desert land, I was halfway to Bhangarh in a hired cab. It began to hit me as to what a Herculean task I had taken up, to unravel a native mystery that had stayed so well hidden for eons. Nevertheless, I set out, all warrior-like, determined to come back with some answers, at least for myself, if not for anyone else.

All along the drive, I thought about the fort. How would it be? What kind of experience lay in store for me? Would I encounter any of the paranormal activity that it was famous for?

When the citadel made its first appearance over the scorched horizon, a cold nervous chill ran down my spine.

Something indefinable happens to you when you are looking at one of the scariest places in the country, probably the world, even if it is broad daylight and even if you are a trained paranormal investigator. These were ruins, just as I had expected them to be, neatly surrounded by the steep Aravalli Hills on three sides, but to say they had a strong personality of their own would be an understatement. There was a stately aura about it which harkened to the rich history it still boasts. Even from a distance, that stern pink colossus dazzled like a shrewd seductress, as if to invite unsuspecting travellers right into its belly.

The cab driver pointed it out and stopped the car. 'Sahib, this is as far as my cab goes. This is the village of Gola Ka Bas around you, and the fort is right ahead. You can see it. About fifteen minutes' walking.' I asked him to take me right up to the fort, but he would not budge. The village was as far as he would go, he repeated. Begrudgingly, I paid him his fare and sent him away.

Now, Gola Ka Bas was hardly a village. I would call it a settlement. As I looked around, I saw people and shops that seemed as if they were caught in some kind of medieval time-warp, for not even the slightest shred of technology had made its foray here. And to top that, living so close to a haunted monument! How must the experience for them be, especially in the nights, when, as one article mentions, the fort weeps with the wailing sounds of a thousand and one spirits? Maybe it's akin to those Hawaiian settlements at the foot of active volcanoes, living under the shadow of a behemoth, so to speak.

Gola Ka Bas looked like a habitat of sculptors, going by the many beautiful marble statues that these people were working on. I approached a few of the locals. I opened conversation by praising their work, but the moment I mentioned the fort, they clammed up. Their friendly eyes assumed a cautious glare that told me in no uncertain terms that they didn't wish to even hear the name of the dreaded thing looming on the horizon, leave alone talk about it.

After some observing, I zeroed in on a middle-aged sculptor sitting in the porch of his thatched hut, chipping away at a statue of the goddess Saraswati. Walking up to him, I complimented him on his craftsmanship, which came naturally because his intricate and graceful artistry deserved praise. The man looked up at me, uneasy and annoyed at first, but when he saw that I was a traveller, he relaxed. Maybe he hoped for a sale.

From this sculptor, I found out why the people were so wary of me. Just three days ago, a young man from the village who worked as a parking attendant for the tourists had found a dead body at the gates of the fort. The body was beaten and bruised, and it was evident that the hapless fellow had died a miserable death. I also learnt that this was not a new occurrence. Bodies were found every few weeks at the foot of the fort. No wonder the people lived in such paranoia.

I gleaned a wealth of information about Bhangarh Fort from that sculptor. Mostly facts I already knew, but hearing them from a local's mouth made a difference. This is what he told me about the native lore.

———

Bhangarh Fort was once the abode of Raja Madho Singh and his wife, Rani Ratnavati, who lived here in the early seventeenth century. At that time, the fort was like a palace, opulent and furnished with the most luxurious of amenities. It accommodated various havelis within its premises and there were even dance performances and other cultural extravaganzas held there that enthralled audiences every evening.

The rani was said to be breathtakingly beautiful. Tales of her beauty spread far and wide. There were many valorous men who would die for just a glimpse of her. But the rani wasn't interested in her admirers; her affections lay elsewhere. She had a special yearning to learn the dark arts. The occult, topics of death and resurrection, of invoking spirits—such things fascinated her and she wanted to learn more. When Raja Madho Singh heard of this, he enlisted the services of a *tantrik* named Singhia to come to the palace to teach his queen the rudiments of black magic.

Ratnavati was a quick learner and Singhia was a knowledgeable teacher, but then the forbidden happened. The teacher fell in deep love with his student, who was a queen and, moreover, a married woman. Singhia knew this love was impossible. So, one day, when the rani's maid was purchasing oil for her bath, Singhia secretly put a charm on it. The charm was such that whoever touched the oil would not be able to resist the advances of the tantrik.

But the plan backfired. The rani knew enough black magic herself to recognize that the oil did not smell as it should. She saw through the evil that was in it. Instead of using it on herself, she poured the oil on the ground.

Late that night, the charm began to work. The oil had touched the ground, and now it was the earth that fell in irrevocable love with Singhia. Boulders of earth broke away from the fort and hurtled down towards Singhia's hut. He realized his undoing moments before the boulders fell upon his chest and crushed him.

But in his dying breath, an enraged Singhia cast an evil spell on Bhangarh Fort and all its residents. He cursed the entire court, the rani, the courtiers and the citizens. He decreed that his rejection by their queen would bring them to their doom.

And indeed, hours later, there was an unexplained natural calamity in Bhangarh. Rocks moved, trees were uprooted, birds and insects fell dead from the skies. Stones holding up the fort came loose and within a few minutes, it nearly turned all to rubble, which is the state in which the fort stands today.

It is said that the rani and her courtiers perished in this blight, and today it is their ghosts that haunt the fort. And the fate of Raja Madho Singh remains unknown to this day, for he was never seen after the day of the catastrophe.

———

It was almost noon when I shook off the after-effects of the sculptor's sordid tale and proceeded towards the ill-famed structure. Knowledge is ammunition, and knowing that tale helped. Usually, exorcising a haunted entity is all about being aware of any injustice that might have befallen the spirits when they were in the realm of the living, and understanding how to resolve that injustice. However, I reminded myself that I wasn't here to exorcise; only to know the truth behind the unliberated souls at the fort if there were any. Holding that thought firmly in mind, I made my way in.

The entry to the fort area is through an iron gate. This is a strong and massive construction, weighing several tons. The passage of time had made it heavier, so much so that part of it was entrenched in the ground. It did not even open fully, leaving merely a slit-like opening for a man to pass through.

Next to the gate is the famed signboard put up by the Archaeological Survey of India (ASI). Without mincing words, the signboard states (in Hindi):

It is forbidden to enter this area before sunset or after sundown.

It is forbidden to bring any livestock within the premises for grazing.

It is forbidden to cause any harm to the kevda trees that are found within the area.

The ASI warning further states that the violation of any of these rules is punishable under the applicable laws. This official warning posted right outside the fort strikes terror into the hearts of the locals as well as the people who visit. It is this signboard that has, in great measure, made Bhangarh famous as an officially spooky destination in India.

I wedged myself into the narrow opening in the gate and entered the premises.

There were a few tourists around the place, mostly keeping to themselves and clicking selfies against the ruins and the backdrop of the Aravallis. I walked in their midst, the only loner among all the tourist groups, and began surveying the place.

When you enter the Bhangarh premises, the first thing you see is an open maidan. When I was there in sweltering May, this ground was barren, but it still held the promise of turning lush with grass in the cooler seasons. Beyond it, I saw a temple. Bhangarh has several temples dedicated to many deities, but this particular temple caught my eye. There was something peculiar about it that I could not put my finger on immediately.

I went in and explored it, taking various pictures and appreciating its architecture. That was when it struck me—there was no idol in this mandir. Nowhere was there any indication that this temple was ever dedicated to a god. There might have been a deity here ages ago; Indian forts were known to have temples of their chief deities within the precincts so that their blessings could be invoked during dire circumstances. In the state that I saw it, however, the temple just seemed sad and forlorn; it was as if even the deity had abandoned the place following its complete ruination at the hands of nefarious black magic.

Something nearby grabbed my attention. There was a weather-beaten platform, on which sat a human figure in an upright posture. I went closer and saw that he was a mendicant, a sadhu dressed in dirty white garb, his eyes closed as if he were in deep meditation. His countenance was a contrast to the other eager faces around; it looked to me as if he belonged to this place in some way.

Before I could go up to him, the sadhu opened his eyes and frowned at me.

'Baba, whose temple is this?' I asked.

He looked skyward, as if even he was looking for an answer.

I tried again. 'Do you come here often?'

He nodded this time. His visage was still forbidding but that nod was warm, even friendly. It prompted me to sit next to him. He did not object.

'I am exploring this place. Can you tell me about it?'

'What do you want to know?'

It was a gruff voice, not quite the mellow voice you'd expect from a holy man.

'Do a lot of tourists come here?'

'These days, yes,' he said in a tone of complaint. 'There was a time when the fort was left alone by people and that was the time of its glory. Now people come with their bags and phones and cameras and spoil the place. They come here looking for whatever they expect and mock and laugh to show they are not afraid, but then . . . as the sun begins to set, they voluntarily vacate the premises. One by one, they go out, all of them. Hypocrites! There are no guards here, no patrollers, nothing. Why would they skitter out like that if there was nothing here?'

'But is it really haunted, baba? Are there spirits here?'

He gave me a withering look and guffawed. 'Haunted! That's what you think?'

'So it is not haunted?'

At that, the sadhu peered deep into my eyes. There was something in that look I could not define. He held my gaze for a moment before replying.

'Haunted, you say? This fort is much more than that. You want to explore this place, do you? Trust me, boy, if you value your life, banish that thought and go back to your comfortable bed, wherever you have come from.'

I kept mum and moved away from the sadhu, turning to look at the citadel itself. The conversation had only steeled my resolve to go seeking. It was as if the fort were calling out to me now.

———

Entering through a smaller door, I came across an area that must have once been a market. There were broken shops with some of their shelves still intact, where maybe wares had been displayed and sold ages ago. Now, they were just relics of a bygone era. I walked on the path flanked by these shops on either side and felt a bizarre kind of synergy. What did they sell? How did the shopkeepers lure their customers? Why did they suddenly go defunct? My observations only reinforced the legend—something sinister had happened here. The structures of these shops were battered, and I could tell it wasn't simply the outcome of weathering over time. It was as if some calamity had broken out here, perhaps when the shopkeepers and customers were still around, and it must have been a massacre that made people run helter-skelter.

Quite a macabre image to conjure up from four centuries ago while standing in the exact same spot.

Crossing the market, I came across a small pond, a rectangular reservoir with stone walls around it. I recalled from my talks with the locals that this used to be the special pond used by Rani Ratnavati herself. It was now covered by an enclosure, but in those days when the queen used it, it might have been more natural, blending in with the surroundings. A few tourists hung around the pond, and I felt drawn to it too.

Sometimes, it is just this intuitive feeling that I get, the kind I got at the marketplace, which tells me that a place once was, or still is, a hub of paranormal activities. There was something about this pond that I could not quite figure out at the moment, but it beckoned to me to find out. As I moved closer, I felt a distinct dip in the temperature. It was suddenly abnormally cold. Outside, the temperature was hovering above 42 degrees Celsius, but when I pointed my thermometer in the direction of the water to check, I was shocked—the temperature here was 12 degrees Celsius.

What's more, the water was crystal clear. To be honest, I haven't seen such clear waters even in the Himalayan streams. That in itself was quite impossible, given the fact that tourists would not have spared any effort in sullying the waters as much as they could.

I didn't know then, but I felt sure that something had happened at this pond. The first thing that a paranormal investigator knows is that an inexplicably low temperature is an indication that something is afoot.

Waterbodies are known to be the special haunts of ethereal beings. I closed my eyes and tried to concentrate. In my experience with the paranormal, I have, at times, displayed better perceptive tendencies than any gadgets have. With the reputation of the fort, I expected to hear weeping wails, abuses and curses, long screeching sounds, which are the kinds of things you hear if you have even a faint connection with the other world. But all I could hear was the rising and falling of the water, which was even melodious in its tranquil rhythm, as if it was trying to sing me a song of an age long gone.

———

It was a little after noon when I finally entered the fort. Walking through the grilled door, I found myself in a long corridor with rooms on either side. These were probably the workers' quarters—where the soldiers and servants lived in those times. Even though that might have been the purpose, they seemed odd to me—these 'rooms' were mere niches, offering barely enough space for one individual. Smaller than most prison cells, really. Plunged in darkness, although it was scorching sunlight outside. Why anyone would build such rooms for their trusted soldiers was beyond my comprehension.

Unzipping my backpack, I took out the heat sensor. This is another quick assessment device we professionals use. It constantly measures the temperature of a place, and if there's a dip below normal values, it immediately catches the fluctuation. Armed with the sensor, I walked ahead, even inspecting some of the rooms. Oddly, there were not many tourists in this part of the fort, barring a handful of the bravest ones.

And so I went from room to room, corridor to corridor, scouring every bit of the place that I could get into. My eye was on my gadget at all times. However, though I scanned the entire fort practically twice over, I found no remarkable variation in the sensor readings.

It was about 5 p.m. when I finished my tour, covering all the levels of the fort. I had not caught anything on my sensor that would count as abnormal, except at one point, when the sensor did behave a wee bit unusually. I followed in that direction and found, on one of the upper floors of the fort, a small shrine. It was the kind of place of worship that people build out of stones. This shrine appeared to be dedicated to Lord Shiva, for I could make out a Shivling–like object. I could not be sure though. And someone had offered prayers there recently, for I found fresh flowers, sandalwood and burnt stubs of incense by the shrine.

I didn't find that too puzzling. We Indians are known to build shrines wherever we go. This looked like something a visitor might have built and then others simply continued with the tradition, for who in their right mind destroys a shrine?

So that was it, I thought. So much for the much-touted haunt that is Bhangarh Fort! Likely overhyped, the same as many other places with similar reputations. This actually set me on the path of a belief that cemented itself in my later exploits—the truly horrific locations are those that are not really known by many people, the lonely and forgotten places. That's where people don't dare to set foot even in broad daylight. A place like Bhangarh, which is much visited in the daytime, cannot be as haunted as they make it out to be.

After hours of searching, my scepticism grew stronger. But there were two things that kept me from leaving the place at that point.

Firstly, there was the ASI signboard. Why would a government body put up such a notice if there really wasn't anything there? Secondly, what about the pond? That was truly bizarre, and even if there was nothing paranormal about the fort itself, the pond was positively screaming for my attention.

Packing up my backpack, I went outside and sat by the pond. I had made up my mind. Having come so far, it would not make sense to go back without some answers. So I would hang around for the night; if something were to happen, it would happen in the envelop of darkness, once these pesky tourists abandoned the place, leaving the coast clear for any unnatural entities that exist here to come out and play.

———

I stayed put by the pond as the sun began to set. And though I had heard about how the entire complex would be empty at sunset, watching it happen was both amusing and foreboding. Even before the lower half of the sun's orb could touch the horizon, most people had vacated the premises. Couples holding hands, groups of friends who had been laughing and giggling all along, even families with their children in tow—everyone bundled out. It was as if they had been expelled by some mysterious force.

Well, that force was fear. Rather, I should say the fear of being afraid. That's what most of our fear boils down to anyway. We aren't really frightened most times, but it is the anticipation of what might happen that makes us react in peculiar ways. And here in Bhangarh, I was seeing that unfold.

By the time the sun fully set, it was 7 p.m. There still was the residual, reflected light, and I kept sitting by the pond to see if anyone would come to shoo me away. Most monuments have a posse of guards tasked with the sole responsibility of driving out tourists at closing time. I waited for about an hour, watching the darkness consume the area in entirety, but no one approached me.

It was almost 8.30 p.m. when I stood up. I had satiated my hunger with some biscuits I had carried along and had my fill of water from the pond (very sweet water, I must say), which revived me enough to continue on my mission.

I had gathered by then that there was practically no way out till morning. No one came here in the night, which meant there was no transport either. Come what may, I had to spend the night at Bhangarh—there was no other option. But, to be frank, the thought gave me a heady feeling, like no intoxication ever could.

Silence is never absolute. Even the late-night stillness of a city carries within it the sounds of honking horns and chattering passers-by and buzzing electricity, if nothing else. Villages are never completely quiet either, for you can hear the sounds of kitchens and small shops, or the rustling trees and nearby domestic animals going about their motions. And then there's the silence of a forest, which is punctuated with the sounds of insects and birds and distant animals; or the silence of an ocean, where you will still hear the waves lashing about languorously, trying to make contact between the earth and the sky. However, the silence that invaded Bhangarh Fort after dark was the kind no human being might ever have experienced. It was the closest to an absolute void, where nothing existed, not even the faintest vibration in the air. And that is where I stood now, with only the sound of my beating heart for company.

I slowly stepped inside once again, taking baby steps, not wanting to disturb the quietude of the atmosphere in the least. If there was anything in here, it must have come out by now, and was probably lurking about somewhere. The last thing I wanted was to become the distraction in a savage animal's nocturnal wanderings.

With a sceptical mind I proceeded, relying on my gadgets to tell me if something was amiss. Fully alert, I came back to the rooms. The fact that I was all alone had heightened my senses. I turned sharply at even the faintest indications of sound, which were mostly on account of my own movements in the desolate ruins.

Pointing my gadgets at different corners of the fort, I walked. There was this feeling of heaviness beginning to creep up on me, but from experience I knew that it was not on account of any fear or even any paranormal activity. Loneliness does that to you. Being lonely is the heaviest burden there is. And, for me, in such cases, any company is welcome. Even spirit company for that matter.

After investigating the place for an hour, I drew a blank. I went into most of the small prison-cell rooms. I roamed the terrace above and checked all the corners. I went to the dance hall where I shut my eyes and stood still for a minute to find if I could sense any of those sounds of merriment from ages ago. I even checked the bathroom where the rani used to bathe. But, no, not a thing. If spirits had made their haunts here, that was probably long ago. Now it appeared to me that even the spirits had abandoned this area, finding their salvation elsewhere.

Finally coming to the acceptance that this was a grand waste of time, I came back to the corridor that would lead me out. There was not even the remotest semblance of any paranormal activity here. It was close to midnight when I started to make my way out. If I was lucky, I thought to myself, I might find some vehicle plying on the road, at least a biker who could give me a lift, though I did not have much hope of that.

I came to the marketplace, my K2 sensor still aimed in the hope of a minor signal somewhere, when I had the first big shock of that night.

It was up there; in one of the rooms on the second floor, there was the light of a burning fire.

The light looked so bizarre from where I was standing that I almost audibly gasped. I was sure I had visited that room just a few minutes ago, and there had been nothing. If I was not mistaken (and I found out later that I was not), this was the same room housing the Lord Shiva shrine I had seen earlier.

The flames appeared to be dancing in the wind, but there was no wind. It was so hot that night that my shirt was sticking to my chest. Not a hint of breeze where I was; but in that window I could see the oranges and yellows and crimsons of the flame beginning to change hues and dance, and as I moved closer, which I did very gingerly, I could even hear the crackling of twigs. Someone—or *something*—had lit a fire in there. The only unnatural thing here was, how could a fire lit using burnt twigs start raging so furiously in barely a few minutes?

I had to investigate this.

I entered the halls again, making as little noise as possible. This time I knew exactly where to go. I stayed as quiet as a mouse in the darkness, keeping to the shadows, and ascended the tall staircase that led to the upper floor. The corridor had been plunged in darkness earlier, so much so that I hadn't been able to see my own hands, but now it was bathed in the orange-yellow light of the flame coming from the room at the end.

Most people might have had a hard time breathing in that dank corridor, as did I. But I kept going. As I took the next few steps, I heard the unmistakable hum of someone mumbling. After a few more steps, I knew this was not just plain mumbling; it was chanting, as in mantras. Someone, or maybe more than one person, was reciting something. Not loudly and clearly, but muttering it under their breath, the syllables barely escaping their lips. But the entire space was so silent that even muttering sounded like a cacophony as it reverberated in that narrow corridor, and it grew sharper as I dared on ahead.

I came to the room and stopped. Restraining myself by staying stuck to the wall now, out of sight of whatever might be inside, I leaned forward so that only my upper torso moved. My head barely poked in then, and what I saw in that room shocked me so badly that I could have keeled over.

Now, I am describing the scene exactly as my fear-ridden mind saw it at first glance.

In that room, on one side of that makeshift shrine, which was burning with bright licks of fire now, were three tantriks. Sitting on the floor, their bare backs to me, they swayed with their eyes shut; I could see slivers of their faces. They had holy ash (*vibhuti*) smeared on their faces, huge *rudraksha* beads hanging around their necks and smaller beads tied as bracelets on their upper arms. In the hands of one of them, who led the other two in the chant and might have been their leader, there was—*believe you me*—a human skull. The skull looked freshly removed from a corpse, for it dazzled in its whiteness; it didn't have that dull-yellow hue of old decomposed skulls. This chief tantrik waved the skull in the air as he chanted, and all three of them jerked and twitched as if they were performing a bizarre, unrehearsed and unchoreographed dance where they sat.

This was enough to make my blood curdle, and it did. I am not scared of spirits and, trust me, I can go to the loneliest place in the world and spend a night there. But these were humans. People in the flesh. And I don't need to tell you this—humans are a million times scarier than any undead creature.

That point proved itself a moment later. There was something else in the room, at the other end, beyond the fire. The flames prevented me from seeing it at first, but the moment I did, I knew I would never be able to unsee that sight for the rest of my life.

It was someone tied to a post. I could see him now, a young man about twenty-two years of age, stripped stark naked, not a thread on his body, his hands and legs wrapped around the post and tied with sturdy ropes. I saw lines of blood on his chest—wounds—and that is when I began to lose control over myself. Just then, the young man's eyes opened and he looked right into my eyes.

The pleading look that I saw in those eyes will haunt me till the end of my days.

Then the most dreadful thing of that night happened. Following the direction of that hapless boy's gaze, the chief tantrik turned. I stood there, transfixed, outlined by the door frame, trapped in the gaze of the tantrik's eyes, like a lone deer caught in the headlights of a furiously approaching vehicle on a highway.

Before I could move a muscle, the tantrik did. He picked something up in an instant reflex and, yelling a highly obscene word, flung it right at me. As it hurtled in my direction, I had a fleeting glimpse of what that thing was—it was the skull he had held in his hands.

———

I have been foolhardy many times, but I thank my merciful stars that this was not one such occasion. For if I had stopped to think even for a second, I would not have been able to tell you this tale. Not from the earthly realm at least.

Even before the skull reached me, the tantrik had stood up. I could see that he was mad as a bull, raging, his nostrils flared, and while the other tantriks continued to sit, he took the lead and charged at me, full force. This is where my innate intelligence took over and ordered me to run. And run I did, in the opposite direction, all along the corridor, my stride causing some of the loose fragments on the walls to collapse and fall.

No, these weren't spirits. These were humans, and as I have told you before, they are the most vicious of all.

The tantrik would disappear behind the walls and then appear again, hurl abuses at me and throw objects. At one point, he even threw a femur at me. I saw it just as it rolled away after hitting me, a sharp jab on my lower vertebrae. I still have the scar as a souvenir from that gruesome night.

My steps weren't as sure-footed as his. He was like a goat in the mountains, for he probably knew the twists and turns of this fort well, but I was clumsy, tripping and falling and getting up, confused about which turns to take. As I ran, flashes of my life ran through my mind. But something deep inside told me this was not going to be the end. I had more things to do in life.

And just as that thought occurred to me, I saw the entrance of the fort, the door that led to the marketplace and the pond, and beyond it, the gate. When I spotted that, I did not turn to look behind me even once afterwards. The tantrik was surely gaining on me; I could even sense his breath on my neck at one point and a faint scraping of the tips of his fingers against my shirt as if he might have almost caught up with me, and I could almost see myself hog-tied, just like that poor boy up there, slashed and tortured for god-knows-what. But that was not my day to die. I found deliverance. I took a last big lurch and was out of the door.

The moment I was out of the fort, the pursuit ceased. I could tell. There was no one chasing me any more. I was in the open ground, the welcoming warm breeze buffeting me on all sides.

———

I have no earthly idea as to how much I might have run that night. Mind you, even outside the fort, I did not stop running. I have never come so close to losing my life. The chants of those tantriks, the wounds on that boy, the feeling of the human bones hitting my body . . . these aren't things that you can get out of your mind so easily.

I kept running on the road outside Bhangarh Fort without knowing where it led to, and I only stopped when I saw a man walking on the road. I was somewhat pleased to see—it was the sadhu I had met earlier that morning.

'So did you see what you shouldn't have?'

His voice soothed me. It wasn't raspy any more, as it had been in the morning; there was a calming quality to it now. I collapsed by his side, right there on the road. Only then did I realize how exhausted I was.

'Wh-what was that, baba?' I asked him.

'If I'd told you in the morning, you wouldn't have believed me. So I have stopped saying it to anyone. Whoever wishes to go in, go by all means. Everyone has to deal with their karma anyway. Yours, my boy, is good. That's why you could escape.'

'But what was that? Who were those people?'

'Long ago, my boy,' the sadhu began, sitting down beside me, 'in the times of Rani Ratnavati, the tantrik Singhia, who had his eye on her, had his eye on something else too.'

I looked up, confused.

'It is in the pond,' continued the sadhu, 'but no one knows exactly where. It is a stone, but no ordinary stone. And that, my son, is the Paras Mani.'

I turned sharply to look at him, so sharply that something in my neck cracked. Of course, I had heard of the Paras Mani, the Philosopher's Stone of Indian lore, the magical stone that could turn even the basest iron into pure gold by its mere touch.

'The tantrik wanted Rani Ratnavati so that he could own her and her fort, and thus the pond itself. He wanted that more than anything else. That's why when the rani spurned him, his curse was so strong.'

'But who are these people?'

'They are the followers of that evil tantrik, descended through many generations. A lot of things have changed about them, but one thing remains the same—they still have the yearning to get their hands on the stone.'

'But the boy?'

'Ah, that boy is as good as dead. He is their sacrifice.'

'What?'

'That's how it is, son. Stray drifters in these lands are picked up by these tantriks and sacrificed at that spot. The tantriks believe that by doing this on certain special nights of a year, they are getting closer to the Paras Mani.'

'So there are no ghosts here? Nothing? What about the signboard by the government? Why don't the government or the villagers stop this?'

'Because . . .' the sadhu placed his hand on mine and said, 'if the tantriks find the Paras Mani, isn't it for the good of all?'

And with those foreboding words still hanging in the night air, the sadhu stood up and left. I called after him, but he wouldn't listen. I ran after him, but he had disappeared in the wilderness surrounding that dirt road.

———

To this day, I have mixed feelings about Bhangarh Fort. Three years have passed since I visited it, and it all feels so surreal to me now. In fact, even as I am writing this, there's a small part of my brain that is wondering if it all really happened. Were there really evil black magicians there, and was I really a witness to a human sacrifice that I could not stop?

I try not to think about it too much. Some things are beyond our control. I have found in my experience that you may be able to control ghosts and spirits, but you can never rein in the evil machinations of the human mind.

The day we control that, we will truly have made our place on this earthly realm that we claim to dominate.

5

The Tragic Ghost of Vas Villa

WHEN I HEARD about Bengaluru's infamously haunted location, Vas Villa, for the first time, I could not wait to explore it. Equipped with practically no tools at the time, just a youthful courageous spirit for adventure and a thirst for the truth, I trespassed into Vas Villa on a lonely summer night. What I found in there was a markedly different aspect of the paranormal. In fact, it would not be wrong to say that my respect for the dead increased manifold after my experience at this tragic site.

Come with me to Vas Villa. But bring with you your nerves of steel. This one is going to challenge you.

In late 2015, I had the occasion to revisit a city I had spent a significant part of my childhood in—Bengaluru. A few of my uncles still call the Garden City their home. They have been living there with their families ever since I can remember. Many of my cousins (I have a large family) have grown up here, though most of them have moved to other parts of the world now. However, in 2015, when one of them got married, it turned into a grand family reunion.

With the entire family gathered in my uncle's palatial house in the upmarket area of Banerghatta, there was a definite promise that this would turn out to be like the stereotypical, big fat Indian wedding that our movies have so often showcased. The thing with family weddings is that the final days in the run-up to the ceremony are as exciting (some would say more exciting) than the wedding day itself. There is no exhilaration greater than having the family arrive piece by piece, meeting long-lost relatives and catching up with them and watching the revelry begin to unfold. Everything is left behind—your bills, your deadlines, your worries—as you treat yourself to this much-needed detox from the outside world and spend time with the people who matter the most.

We too were having our bit of unbridled fun. I hung around with the youngsters, mostly all my cousins. None of the elders policed us as we spent night after night awake, chatting, eating, playing cards. When the evenings wore down and the dinners were done, we practically had the humungous house to ourselves.

It was on one such evening, the eve of the engagement ceremony, that I first heard about Vas Villa. We were in the main hall of the house, playing cards, gossiping and singing. There was a lot of ruckus, and I sat in the midst of it all, oblivious to the existence of the intriguing Vas Villa, about which I would soon find out in the next few minutes.

The TV was on, though it was muted. No one was watching it anyway; they were too engrossed in their own thing. I happened to glance at the screen. A local channel was airing a late-night news report. The visuals were of a derelict house that had the air of long-lost opulence. There was a caption running below, but it was in Kannada, a language I cannot read. From the looks of it, they were showing a haunted spot.

Immediately, I turned up the volume. But the reportage was also in Kannada. The stills then switched over to some video footage. It showed two people with torches walking through the corridors of the house. The way they were walking and reporting, pointing their cameras at various places of the house, I knew right away that it was the footage of a paranormal investigation.

My cousin Vicky, who knew and always supported my paranormal leanings, came up to me. He still lived in Bengaluru. I asked him to explain what he was seeing. In a playful manner, he began translating simultaneously the lines being spoken on the screen by the investigators.

'So here we are, on this very hot summer night, in this haunted house in Bengaluru. It is called Vas Villa. This here is the main hall . . . and those are the stairs that we are going to climb up in a while. What lies up there? Wait . . . was that a sound behind us? Stay with us as we find out the answer to this frequently asked question—*Is Vas Villa still the abode of its deceased owner, Mrs Dolce Vas?*'

A commercial break came on.

'Should I translate the ads too?' Vicky asked, being the idiot he likes to be.

'Arré, Vicky! Tell me more about this Vas Villa. You have a haunted house right here in Bengaluru and you never told me? Where is this house exactly? What's the story behind it?'

'Oh, hold on! Hold on!' Vicky protested. 'Don't fire so many questions all at once. I know how you get your highs from dead dudes and dudettes, but wait . . .'

'Okay, tell me what you know.'

We went across to one corner of the hall and occupied two chairs, away from the rest of the cousins.

'Vas Villa is our famous local spooky house,' Vicky began. 'A few years ago, two sisters used to live there, Vera Vas and Dolce Vas. Both spinsters. Old, in their late seventies. So one night, Dolce Vas gets murdered in the house. Robbery, I think. Vera Vas leaves the house and never returns. And the posh house falls into the broken-down state that you just saw it in.'

'Oh, she was murdered? That's sad. It may really be haunted then. Dissatisfied spirits are very much attached to the place where they met their death. Have you heard anything about it?'

'There are rumours that Dolce Vas can sometimes be seen walking around in the compound of the house,' said Vicky. 'I mean, you don't see her as her—she's a ghost for God's sake!—but people claim it is her. Same height, hairdo, dress.'

'Have you met anyone who has seen her?'

'No. But the rumours are strong. There are other things too.'

'Like?'

'Noises heard in the house at night. Like people struggling inside. Being suffocated and whimpering. A particular light blinks on and off. People say it was the same place where Dolce Vas used to sit and read in the late evenings. And . . . and . . .' His excitement rose. 'There's this car in the compound of the house. It suddenly starts and begins to purr for no reason, as if someone is trying to take it for a drive.'

I took it all in. To be honest, all that information had brought about a radical shift in my emotional state. Moments ago, I was participating in all the wedding revelry in the house, but now I had this strong urge to get away. Even as Vicky was telling me all those things, a part of my mind began to visualize the empty halls and corridors of the house as they might be at that point of time, the silence that prevailed there, the beautiful cloud of gloom and despair that the house had been plunged in. Call me weird, but in that moment, the tragic story of the abandoned villa held more appeal to me than the festivities going on in the house.

I told Vicky what I thought. 'Vicky, man, I want to go see Vas Villa right now.'

He did not reply immediately. Any other cousin of mine would have talked me out of it right away, but not Vicky. He has been my partner in crime on a few occasions; for instance, when we used to go check out desolate places as children. Life took him in a different direction, but those days had forged a connection between us, a shared bond over a common love for the paranormal.

'Hey, Rummy, I won't be able to tear myself away at this time, and even you shouldn't. It's a *shaadi ka ghar*, man!'

Rummy is my nickname within the family. When they call me by that name, I feel like I am really home.

'No one will miss me. I'll go now.'

'Why do you have to go tonight itself?' Vicky said. 'See, the engagement is tomorrow. Then we have a day's break till the wedding. You can go tomorrow night.'

I was disappointed. He saw that.

'Okay,' he relented. 'I know how crazy you get about paranormal stuff. It won't be a good idea to have you brooding all the time during the engagement tomorrow. Do one thing. You go alone. I will take care of things here if anyone asks.'

'You'll really do that?'

'Of course,' he said. 'And let me see if I can arrange for my friend James to take you.'

'James? He's that tall fellow with the Scorpio, right?'

'Yes. He can drive you there. Vas Villa is on St Mark's Road, which is about an hour's drive from here. It's better if you have some kind of transport to come back from there in the middle of the night.'

'He'll do that for me?'

'Not you. But he'll do that for me,' Vicky said with a laugh.

I turned my attention back to the visuals on the TV screen while he made the call. Yes, it was a paranormal investigation. Pre-recorded footage. Even without understanding what they were saying, I could say that these people were rank amateurs from the way they were going about the exploration. They carried sticks in their hand. Sticks! And using those, they were prodding at various spots on the wall. They were shouting as if to call whatever entity might be there.

112

Here, I need to make a note for my readers. This is definitely not the way to go about an investigation. We have to be respectful of the other world. Since they are not living any more, it is easy to forget that they too were humans once, just like you and me. Prodding about with sticks and uncaringly making a noise in their abode is tantamount to mocking them. A spirit, if it exists in that place, would never condone this kind of activity.

Vicky got off his call. He was smiling. 'Yes, James will take you there.'

'That's great!'

'Yeah. You are going to have a grand time during the drive too. James is full of local stories. Ask him anything about Vas Villa!'

———

I left with James at around 11.30. My cousins protested, but Vicky took care of it, probably telling them that I had to go with James to make some last-minute arrangements for the wedding reception. I left the house as quickly as I could, carrying with me just the bare minimum equipment, and got into James's waiting car.

James turned out to be quite a chatty and forthcoming person. He already knew the purpose of my nocturnal mission. I had to ask him but once and he was ready with the story of the Vas sisters. I knew part of it already, but his insight proved to be of great help. From his story, I could piece together the history of Vas Villa.

Vas Villa was a beautiful bungalow built by E.J. Vas, an advocate at the Bombay High Court, back in 1943. It was one of the many charming villas that dotted the cityscape, standing solemnly in its peaceful neighbourhood. E.J. Vas bequeathed the bungalow to his two daughters, Vera and Dolce. Neither of his daughters ever married, so they had no families of their own. Vera, the older daughter, was a teacher, while Dolce was a piano instructor. Dolce particularly loved the house. She was the one who had decorated it, and since she spent more time in the house, she had a strong attachment to everything it contained. The sisters lived a tranquil life in complete harmony with the neighbours for many years to come.

It was much later in their lives that tragedy befell them. Dolce had just turned seventy-five. On the evening of 4 September 2002, Dolce was alone at home. Unknown to her, a burglar had been monitoring the house, and he took this opportunity to break in. No one knows what exactly happened, but probably the burglar panicked on seeing a person in the house he expected to be empty. A minor scuffle followed, which ended in the murder of Dolce Vas.

When Vera came home, she was shocked beyond belief. Her only companion in the world had been snatched away in such a heartless and brutal manner.

A probe soon followed and a case was filed. But most unfortunately, nothing came of it. The burglar was never apprehended. Though the case became quite a local sensation, it was never solved.

What happened after that was much more tragic. It is said that the day Dolce died, Vera left the house and never returned afterwards. She left the villa exactly as it was, not touching even a single piece of furniture that belonged to the house. It was as if she knew that Dolce would not approve of her house being disturbed, just as she had been when alive. In fact, Vera even left behind their car, a Hillman Minx, which was in good shape back then.

In a way, she converted the house into a mausoleum for her sister, freezing her last moment in time, so to speak.

This much was about the crime and its aftermath. Now, as we journeyed towards the villa, James delved into the stuff that I wanted to know about more. With a little prodding, I got him to tell me about the legend built around this house.

There is a firm belief among the locals that Dolce Vas never left the house, and they mean it in quite a literal sense. So there it is then—a lot of people are firmly convinced that Vera Vas buried her sister somewhere on the property itself.

I'll be frank—that bit was hard to take. It might sound impractical as to how a woman might be able to bury her sister who was the victim in a crime investigation, but stranger things are known to happen. To speak of Vera, she was never seen again. No one knows where she went. Maybe she died, maybe she moved, no one will ever know for sure.

This only reinforces people's belief that the strange apparitions of a woman they see around the house are of none other than Dolce Vas. In fact, on some evenings, passers-by have heard the faint strains of a piano playing inside the house.

———

It was around 1.30 a.m. when James parked the car on the opposite side of the street. I continued to sit in the car for a while, taking in the complete structure. Somehow, I felt this strong pull from the house, calling me in. Taking a deep breath, as I prepared to get out of the car, I asked James, 'Won't you come along?'

'No, bro!' he said. 'I have brought you till here. Now it is you and the house.'

Curious, I asked him, 'Are you afraid of the stories? If you do wish to come, come. You are with me. You are safe.'

'I don't want to take the risk,' James said in a firm tone. 'You go ahead. I will be parked at the corner of the street.'

'But it might take me a couple of hours.'

'It does not matter. I will be waiting.'

I did not insist further. As he drove away, I clutched my bag of equipment tighter and walked towards the gate.

Vas Villa stood majestically on St Mark's Road in complete defiance of its dilapidated state. It was in stark contrast to the other residential villas on either side of it, houses that were peopled by happy families leading their happy lives. It was a silent neighbourhood though, or maybe it was just that hour of the night when families retire to bed. Apart from the stray barking of dogs, it was quiet.

Even in the moonlight, I could see that the walls were in ruin. Sections of the house were falling apart. Those walls might have been white once upon a time, but now they bore the colour of disregard. Keeping me away from the building was a white wall that ran all along the property. There was a black iron gate that was firmly shut, secured by a lock with a chain. It was as if whatever was in there did not want to be disturbed.

Looking in through those rods, I got a better idea of the layout of the house, and to me, it looked all the more inviting. I could see the portico right out front. And under the portico stood the Hillman Minx of the Vas sisters, in a state of abject neglect. That beautiful car reduced to such a dismal condition was a metaphor for the deterioration of the entire house and its inhabitants. There was something poignantly sad about the whole thing.

Averting my gaze, I could see the windows. From the little light that passed in, I could see that the furniture was still in there. The room was witness to the stories born around this place. It seemed to have a life of its own, having absorbed the life of its deceased owner who loved it so much.

I felt compelled then to do something that I did not really want to—I decided to scale the wall and gain entry into the house. I somehow felt that the house was calling out to me, and I had only this one chance to see it for myself.

Looking carefully to make sure that no one was watching me, I stood by the white peripheral wall and, on a silent count of three, quickly jumped in, landing on my feet. I was inside the property. And I could see the worn-out marble plaque that read: *E.J. Vas, 1943*.

The feeling that I was in a place that might be a crypt for a much-loved woman hit me hard right about then.

———

I started with the Hillman Minx first, the car in which Dolce Vas might have spent a considerable amount of her time. Up close, I could see it was a complete wreck with not much that could possibly be salvaged. But there was still a stately air about it. Its owner must have considered it a prized possession at one time.

I tried the door of the car, and it opened. It was so worn out that the locks had given away.

Opening the door and worrying that it might just fall off its hinges, I crept into the car. There was a layer of dust all over and I had to cover my nose. I got my K2 meter out and started probing around, giving the different parts of the car a once-over. There wasn't anything out of the ordinary. Close to the dashboard, the frequency spiked. But that was unsurprising; stray magnetic fields abound near it.

Something on the dashboard grabbed my attention—a doll figurine hanging from the mirror. This was a plastic doll, dangling away thus for years. I blew the dust away. The eyes stared back at me. Even in that state of disrepair, that doll was so lifelike. At least in those eyes, there was an expression that left no question of the pain it might have endured.

I stilled myself and said, 'Dolce . . . Mrs Dolce Vas? Are you here?'

There was no activity on the K2 meter.

It was all so sad.

———

After spending ten minutes inside the car, I decided to venture into the house itself. I came up to the main door and found it secured with another huge lock. There was no way to get in through there. I began looking around for some other way, and then my gaze fell upon one of the windows on the side of the house. The glass was broken near the bolt. I guessed it to be the work of some miscreants who might have broken into the house sometime.

As I thrust my hand through that hole and unlatched the deadbolt, I had the feeling that I was doing something that might land me in trouble. But I calmed my conscience and moved on. Though I was trespassing, I had noble intentions. I let my curiosity rule over me that night.

The place where I landed looked like the main hall of the house. It was the same room that I had seen earlier through the other window from the gate. An architect might have marvelled at the large space contained in here, and would even see through all the dilapidation everywhere. But all I could see at that point was decay. The furniture still stood in the place where it might have all those years ago, but in such a state that even a junk dealer would not find any use in the items. A huge frayed and worn sofa dominated the room. There were chairs coated in an inch of dust, so much so that you could not tell the original colour of their upholstery. I looked at the ceiling for electrical fittings. The fans were gone, probably taken away by burglars. Their bare rods miserably jutted out of the ceiling. The light holders were all there, but the lights were missing.

Bleak as the whole situation was, I told myself that this was the perfect abode for someone who was meant to have left the earthly realm but hadn't yet.

My primary intention was to see whether Dolce Vas was indeed buried somewhere on the property, either in the house itself or in the compound outside. Vas Villa was supposedly a mausoleum for its last resident—I wanted to either confirm or debunk that theory. If she was here, and even if Vera had left her grave unmarked, there would be some sign of her presence. This was a time when I needed my paranormal equipment the most.

The presence of a grave would have cemented the fact that Dolce was here. While it wouldn't constitute irrefutable proof of her spectral presence, it would mean that this was indeed her last resting place. The least I hoped to find was a grave, but as it turned out, I ended up seeing much more than that.

Armed with my K2 meter, I began to monitor different areas of the house. The hall was most likely where Dolce might be if she was indeed in the house, but I could find nothing, not even the stray fluctuation. I moved to other areas. The kitchen was next, but that too was devoid of any activity. There was a bedroom on the ground floor. Again nothing. A flight of stairs led to the upper storey of the house. There were two bedrooms there and a gallery facing outwards. I scanned every area here, and even looked for any visual clues, such as a marking or a difference in the floor tiles, but I made no discoveries whatsoever.

After spending close to an hour inspecting the house, I stood in the gallery and looked at the world outside—the world as Dolce Vas might have seen it at times on her lonely evenings. It was a residential colony, perfect for aged spinsters to call a home. The houses were upmarket and they probably housed well-to-do families. I could picture Dolce and Vera mingling with these kind folk with common courtesies and minding their own business. Standing there, I felt a swell of grief. Why would someone kill a woman who had harmed no one? Just for a little bit of money. Is that fair? Did Dolce deserve such a death, and Vera such a decline from her happy state of life? Is the divide between the rich and the poor so bad in our world that they provoke such crimes?

Anyway, I struck out. This seemed to be just another abandoned villa. I had found nothing ghostly about it thus far. In fact, I could sense a certain positive energy about the house, something that told me that despite what had happened in the house, the residents were now at peace.

Thinking that I had at least some answers now, if only for myself, I turned from the gallery to walk down the stairs and exit the house. It was then that I had the startling experience that had been waiting for me.

I was back in the corridor of the first floor, making my way from the gallery to the stairs. My movements were slow and heavy; my mind was overflowing with thoughts of the life that had once been lived here. For some reason, I thought of a cat. Did the Vas sisters have a cat? Were they cat ladies? Or maybe they had a dog? When Dolce was murdered and Vera abandoned the house, what happened to the pet? Vera might not have been in a frame of mind to think about the pet. Did she leave the animal behind and did it get locked in? Or maybe it ran out somewhere, shocked in its own animalistic way about everything that had happened.

I was overthinking, I know, but move around in a silent house that has been empty for years and such thoughts will assail you. The nerves of our mind that are susceptible to the bizarre thrive in darkness and silence.

I was still ridden with such thoughts, when a soft thud made me jump.

For a moment, I was disoriented. I waited breathlessly—had that sound been a part of my imagination too? As I stood absolutely still, I heard the thud again.

Soft and slow, like an animal jumping from a height on to the floor.

No, I told myself, it was not an animal. My mind was overworking as usual. I was picturing an animal just because I had been thinking of an animal.

But what if it was? What if they really had a pet that had been locked in all these years? That animal must be feral by now, baying for anything to eat, baring its fangs.

I made slow progress. The sound had come from one of the bedrooms and I had to pass them on my way to the stairs. Bracing myself, I took a few more steps.

When I came to the bedroom door, I froze.

It was on one of the walls. Against the moonlight, there was a distinct shadow on the wall. I could see it, clearly silhouetted. It had the contours of a woman.

But the thing that made my mouth run dry was—there was no one in the room.

It was a shadow without a source.

The K2 meter was blinking now. Four lights. This was significant. I felt a cold chill overcoming me. As silently as I could, I took out my temperature sensor. Keeping my hands as steady as I could, I aimed the sensor at the shadow and then I lowered my eyes to observe the reading, and then compared it against the temperature in the corridor.

There was a distinct drop of 2 degrees inside the room. I controlled myself.

'Dolce, is that you?' I asked.

As I have said before, the thing with apparitions is that you have to show no fear. If you are frightened, the spirits will feed on your fear, even if they are good entities. I had to make sure I stayed steady in that moment.

I asked more clearly, 'Dolce, are you still in this house?'

There was a faint movement in the shadow. It was barely discernible. I'd not have noticed it if I hadn't been watching so closely. There was a flicker of movement again. It was at the throat. I saw it move.

I knew what it was—it was a gulp, the kind we make when we are swallowing. Behind me, the wooden floor was creaking. It felt as if someone else was walking behind me. I didn't dare to turn as my eyes were fixed on the shadow in front. Slowly, I lowered my eyes and saw that the thermometer was registering a further drop.

'Dolce,' I said, 'what happened with you was brutal. It was an unforgivable offence. No apology is enough. I hope you find your rest in eternal peace. Goodbye, Dolce. I shall now leave.'

As respectfully as I could, I backed away from the room. Once out of sight of the shadow, I turned to look behind.

There was nothing. The creaking had stopped too. The room was filled with clear moonlight again.

My work here was done. I put the equipment into my bag, turned and walked to the window I had come from. I climbed out of it and, just as silently, I walked to the wall and hopped off it.

When I crossed the iron gate, I had a feeling someone was watching me from one of the glass windows of the house.

————

This incident was one of my very first concrete encounters with the paranormal. I was quite a novice then, and though I had the technical knowledge required to deal with such experiences, I did not have the emotional make-up for it. When I saw the ghost of Dolce Vas—and I become surer with each passing day that that was precisely what I saw—I did not know how to react. I did not know what to tell her so that she could find peace. It was a good thing that the spirit was kind and compassionate in life, and it retained those qualities in death.

Vas Villa does not exist now. A few years ago, the house was purchased by a builder and torn down. Nothing of the house remains any more. And no grave or anything of the sort was unearthed.

But the tragic story of Dolce Vas continues. She might be there on St Mark's Road somewhere, walking in the silence of the night. At the very least, she is firmly etched in my mind, and I like to believe that it was she who made me more sensitive to the nature of all beings supernatural.

6

Mayong, the Birthplace of Black Magic

OF THE MANY diverse lands that India is blessed with, the small village of Mayong in Assam is sure to catch the fascination of an intrepid paranormal sleuth. It carries the incredible tag of 'India's Black Magic Village', and it is exactly as it sounds—an entire village where everyone is a practitioner or believer in black magic. In fact, some people also claim that this is the birthplace of all black magic in India, perhaps even the world.

To find out the truth for myself, I paid a visit to Mayong, albeit in a highly sceptical frame of mind. What lay in store for me there was an unparalleled experience that made me question several aspects of my own beliefs. But what is the truth behind this land of illusions? What is the secret of the black magic practised here? I'd never have got the answers if I hadn't visited Mayong, and now I share those experiences with you.

In the summer of 2016, three of us friends—Alok, Jaimeet and I—planned a trip to Guwahati, the largest city in India's north-eastern state of Assam. None of us had been to this idyllic side of our country before, and owing to our busy schedules back home, we had only four days on hand.

Being the most adventurous of the three, I wanted to explore the unfamiliar city as much as I could. My friends wanted to use the time for rest and rejuvenation. That was fine by me, but it meant that I found myself touring the city alone a lot of the time. During one such expedition, I found out about Mayong.

It was on the second morning of our trip that I happened to ask our hotel manager, a tall man named Biswas, for a list of places I could see around the city. He named a few touristy spots, but they did not catch my fancy. Not wanting to tax his patience further, I asked him pointedly, 'Are there any haunted places nearby that I could explore?'

There, I had said it. I hadn't planned to be so direct, but it did not surprise me. It went perfectly with my nature. For a few years now, I had been noticing that wherever I travelled, I invariably ended up finding out more about the paranormally active places in the vicinity. And I would only rest after a trip to that place, howsoever short the time spent there might be.

Biswas looked me up and down. 'That's a strange request,' was all he said.

'I am a paranormal investigator,' I explained. I described briefly the kind of work I did, and my stints with podcasts and television shows. I also told him that I intended to compile my experiences in the varied haunted places of India into a book.

I don't think he understood much, but his ears pricked up at the mention of a book. 'In that case,' he said, 'you should consider making a trip to Mayong.'

Honestly, before that I had not heard this name.

'How have you never heard of it?' Biswas looked shocked. 'Mayong is the village of black magic. Everyone knows magic there and you can see it happen in front of your eyes. You should surely visit the place.'

I could not wrap my head around it at first. Village of black magic? My senses were instantly on alert.

'Sounds intriguing!' I couldn't have feigned the enthusiasm. 'Where do I find this place?'

'It is actually not far from here,' said Biswas. 'Just 40 kilometres away, close to the Pobitora Wildlife Sanctuary. But there is a problem.'

'What?'

'The people of Mayong are a close-knit society. They are also an isolated kind of people. They do not like foreigners on their land.'

I knew what 'foreigners' meant in that context. For simple villagers, the land they inhabit is their only world. Anyone who does not belong to their land is foreign.

'But I am sure there will be some way for me to visit,' I insisted. 'Maybe if I assured them that I just want to see them at work and not do any harm? Just think about it—it will be a great addition to my book. You might find a mention too.'

Biswas gave me another of his long looks. He worked something out in his head and made an odd clucking sound.

'All right, I could help you go to Mayong.'

'Tell me.'

'The current headman of the village is a man named Rinchen, who is coincidentally also a tourist guide. In fact, he sources most of his customers from our hotels here in Guwahati. He should be visiting here tomorrow. I am sure there will be no problem if you hire him as your tour guide.'

'Excellent!' I beamed. After quizzing him for a few more details, I took his leave. I had never used a tour guide before. But from what I heard from Biswas, I believed such a person would be a valuable resource for me to learn about the unfamiliar territory that I was stepping into.

———

I spoke with my friends that night. I told them about Mayong, emphasizing the 'village of black magic' bit, and asked if they wished to accompany me. Their reactions came as a surprise to me. They were terrified! They vociferously made it clear that they didn't want to have anything to do with a place full of black magic.

Now, my beliefs on the subject are somewhat unconventional. Black magic, on the whole, is highly prevalent in India. Not just in the rural areas, as most would think, but even in the cities. You'll find most shops have a lemon–chilli charm hanging above the doorway. That's part of the superstitious lore that comes from black magic. Up until then, my stand on it had always been ambivalent, for I hadn't experienced it all that much. I didn't subscribe to it, nor did I detest it. But one thing's for sure—black magic cannot be denied in paranormal science, especially in India where it is so evident. And my experiences in Mayong, as you shall read ahead, brought me to a definitive conclusion on the matter.

I shared my thoughts with Alok and Jaimeet. I told them not to set much store by black magic practices. They are deliberately made to look scary, but that's only a ploy to attract people and stifle any questions they might ask. I told them to tag along; nothing would happen. But all my powers of persuasion were no match for their preconceived notions and fell on deaf ears. The two wouldn't budge.

I remained firm in my choice. I planned to set out for Mayong with Rinchen when he visited the next morning.

———

Rinchen turned out to be a short-statured man with a fair complexion and a shockingly white beard. He had deep-set brown eyes that seemed to be in a perennial state of laughter. He had the kind of pleasant face you'd be glad to see first thing in the morning. He came to the hotel at exactly 9 a.m., as expected.

Biswas called me to the lobby as soon as Rinchen turned up. He had evidently been briefed about my request, for as soon as he saw me, he asked if I was Jay Alani. I shook his hand and formally introduced myself.

He replied simply, 'So you want to see our village Mayong?'

I nodded.

'You are coming as a tourist?'

I was about to go into the real reason for my interest in Mayong, when Biswas made a gesture to interrupt me. I got the hint. These were simple people, proud of their village and community; any talk of what I really intended to do, which was to investigate them, would be met with a great deal of scepticism. So instead I said, 'Yes. I wish to see the practices that you people perform in Mayong. They sound very fascinating to me.'

'Oh yes! Mayong is a fascinating place!' Rinchen echoed with obvious pride. 'Come then, are you ready to leave now?'

I nodded. I had my backpack ready.

'You will need cash everywhere. Our little Mayong has not gone digital yet!' He laughed.

I smiled, though I wondered what the cash would be needed for. I paid Rinchen upfront for his service and we set out in his vehicle, a much-battered white SUV.

The road was in good shape and it would take us a couple of hours to reach our destination. I used the time to ask my guide as much as I could about this unique village. That conversation itself turned out to be quite remarkable.

The word 'Mayong' comes from the Sanskrit word 'maya', which means 'illusion'. That seems to be the reason behind the name of the village, but there are other theories too. One suggests that the name of the city was obtained from the Moirang tribe, which hails from the nearby state of Manipur. The name may also have stemmed from the phrase *'Maa er ongo'*, which roughly translates as 'part of the Mother', where 'Mother' refers to Goddess Kamakhya from whom black magicians are believed to derive their powers. In fact, there's an old temple of Goddess Kamakhya near Guwahati, which is a prime tourist attraction today.

Historically, Mayong's oldest mention is probably in the Mahabharata itself. This was the abode and later dominion of Ghatotkacha, the son of Bhima with the rakshasi Hidimba. Ghatotkacha derived his magical powers from the forests surrounding Mayong. He used it in great measure when he fought on the side of the Pandavas in the Kurukshetra war and decimated the Kaurava army.

There is another popular historical allusion to Mayong. In 1337, a Mughal king named Muhammad Shah tried to invade Assam. He sent forth an enormous army of 1 lakh horsemen. Under such a massive threat, Assam's fall was inevitable. But as fate would have it, not one of the soldiers ever made their way to Assam. This is a veritable enigma, as the entire army disappeared without a trace while crossing Mayong. No one ever saw any of them after that. The locals still believe that the powerful magic pervading the land led to the annihilation of the whole force.

As we drove on, Rinchen told me more about what happens in Mayong.

'For an outsider like you, things might seem bizarre, but for local Mayong people, nothing is bizarre. Black magic is not just a part of our culture, it drives our economy too. You will see that people from all over come to Mayong to get their problems solved. And our black magicians are really strong. Through their sorcery, they can do incredible things.'

'Like making people rise in the air?'

'That's nothing for them,' Rinchen said in the same proud voice. 'These people can transform others into animals and birds. They can make themselves invisible. They can transport themselves to any place in the universe in the blink of an eye.'

'Will they do all that today?'

Rinchen shook his head. 'It's not that simple.'

'Why?'

'Because these things are not done publicly now.'

'What do you mean by *now*?'

Rinchen turned to look at me, completely ignoring the road ahead. 'Look, in earlier times, such feats were possible because of a certain power the babas got from Maa Shakti. You know what they say—every baba here has a resident ghost in their body.'

My interest was suddenly piqued. 'Really?'

'Yes. I am not trying to frighten you. Our babas have the ability to tame ghosts. They keep them like domestic pets and use them to do their magical work.'

'So you can see these ghosts?' I asked innocently.

'No, only the babas can see them. They talk with them too.'

'You mean to say this is practically a whole village of possessed people? How interesting! And how do they get the ghosts to reside in them?'

Rinchen did not answer right away. After about a minute, he said, 'That happens after a *narbali*.'

'*Narbali*? What's that?'

'Human sacrifice.'

I let out a soft whistle in amazement. A brief silence reigned between us.

Then Rinchen said, 'I don't know about now, but earlier it definitely used to happen. Of course, who knows what happens in the deep dark jungles? The babas that you see in the village are just a few who live the public life. There are stories that there are hundreds and hundreds of them who stay hidden in the heart of the forest, who are never seen and who still carry out the age-old practices. I hope I am not scaring you too much. I don't tell all tourists this kind of stuff, but you look strong. You look like you can take it.'

I heard him out in silence. The only thing that scared me at that moment was the man's utter belief in what he was telling me.

———

We reached Mayong in the heat of the afternoon. The natural landscape of the place turned out to be quite different from what I had expected—verdant lush greenery and well-maintained roads ran through it. Rinchen explained to me that the natural bounty of the place was on account of the Brahmaputra River, on whose banks it lies. This abundance seeped into the natives' lifestyles as well.

I was told there were around 400 families here, and the people I saw seemed generally content and casual. Unlike what I've found in other rural areas in India, I didn't see anyone lazing around despite the afternoon sun. Everyone seemed to be engaged in some activity. I noticed several woodworking shops.

Rinchen informed me that it was the most common local staple occupation.

We stopped at a couple of small temples. These had local deities too, most of them unknown beyond this realm but held in great reverence here. Going by the number of people coming to pay obeisance, I gathered that were a deeply religious people.

Rinchen stopped the SUV in front of a typical simple rural hut made of stone and brick, with a thatched roof. It had a small yard out in front, just an open space covered in mud.

'This is it,' he said as he stepped out. Leaving my backpack in the vehicle, I followed him into the hut.

I expected it to be the home of a family, but it turned out to be something else. Inside were four babas with various sacred marks on their bodies and long chains of *rudraksha* beads around their necks. Their bodies were covered with simple pieces of cloth and they were sitting cross-legged on the floor. They didn't even turn to look when we entered the room. I assumed that they were steeped in some kind of meditation.

Rinchen whispered to me that a puja was going on and that I should wait.

We sat without moving for a few minutes, and then the baba in the centre, who also appeared to be the oldest of them all, opened his eyes.

'What do you seek?' he asked.

I was unnerved by the dispassionate way he said the words. Before I could gather my wits, Rinchen said with the grin of a tout, 'This man has come from Guwahati to see your work, baba.'

'Let him speak for himself,' the baba said.

At that, I sat on the ground next to the baba, somewhat awkwardly. I told him, 'I have heard a lot about the powers of this land of Mayong. I want to know more.'

'What do you want to know?'

'What kind of powers do you have? What are they used for?'

The baba looked at me for a long time before replying.

'Sit down comfortably.'

I eased myself into a comfortable position, crossing my legs.

'You see,' he began, 'Mayong is the land of black magic. Our powers come from nature and from our Maa Shakti. We use these powers for the betterment of mankind.'

'Baba, some people think that black magic is used to do harm,' I said meekly.

'Nonsense!' he shouted. 'That's what gives black magic a bad name. They should come here and see what we do. We use our powers for healing purposes.'

'What kind of healing purposes?'

'Anything! There is no ailment our tantra cannot cure. We can make an impotent man become a father and restore sight to the blind. We can cure all diseases. Sexual diseases. Even cancer and AIDS. But enough talk. Are you here with a purpose?'

I fumbled for words.

'We are not here for empty talk, son.'

'What should I do, sir? I really want to see these marvels happening.' To be honest, I was taking everything the baba said with a pinch of salt, but I was curious to see how far it could go.

The man made a face, as if considering my request. Then he said, 'There are two ways.'

'What are they?'

'Either you wait for a sufferer to come, or you tell me about something you are suffering from.'

It was my turn to consider. 'Do you get people here often?'

'We get a lot of them, but there is no regularity.'

There was no guarantee that someone might turn up while I was there, I thought to myself, but I did not want to miss out on the chance of seeing the baba at work either. After a bit of a mental wrangle, I thought of coming up with a problem for him to solve. And when I say 'coming up', I mean it literally, because I totally fabricated the problem.

This is what I said.

'Baba, there's a man who used to be my friend. He borrowed one lakh rupees from me five years ago and hasn't returned it since. Can you make me get my money back?'

The baba rolled his smoky eyes. 'Is that all? It's quite a trivial problem. Don't you have any ailment?'

'No. I am totally fit.'

'All right then! I will get your money back. It will cost you 1100 rupees.'

'Oh!' I said, and looked at Rinchen. But he was just sitting in a corner, smiling back at me. The amount wasn't much in terms of what I expected to see in return. I reached into my wallet and took out the crisp notes.

The baba's eyes momentarily wandered to the money before they resumed their characteristic listlessness. One of the younger babas sitting behind him, probably his assistant, took the money from me.

The baba said, 'Describe the man.'

I came up with a description promptly. 'He must be twenty-seven now. His name is Amar Trivedi, a resident of Delhi.'

'How does he look? Give me all details.'

'He is around 5'8". Fair. Brown eyes. Straight hair. Has a mole on his chin.' I was actually surprised at how creative I could get.

The man did not respond. He turned and made a gesture to the others around him and they rose with a sense of purpose, as if to carry out some tasks they had been assigned. They went to the back of the hut and came back with several vessels filled with what looked like clay. They set these on the ground and, scooping out dollops of the clay, began to shape something. It was astounding when the shape began to take form. They were making a replica of the man I had just described, and it was really fascinating to see how quickly and expertly they were working at it. It was like watching professional artisans at work.

One of them scooped into another vessel and took out some kind of white powder. With that, he made a circle on the ground right in front of the main baba. He arranged some twigs in it. I realized that they were building a pyre.

What happened next was totally unexpected. The baba reached into a bag that lay by his side and brought out a round object. A human skull! I sat watching, filled with astonishment and a little bit of fear.

He placed the skull in the middle of the pyre, on top of the twigs. He produced a small box next, out of which he took out a bit of red powder, evidently sindoor. He smeared this sindoor on the forehead of the skull. The minor babas then decorated the pyre with stones and flowers, again in a circular manner.

I took out my phone to take a picture. This was something I wanted to record for posterity. Almost instantaneously, I felt a hand slapping mine. It was Rinchen, wagging an index finger at me. I slowly thrust the phone back into my pocket.

It was all set then. The main baba lit the pyre and the rites began. He started a chant, which was low at first and slowly went up by notches in both intensity and volume. I could not make anything of it, for the language was unknown to me. The baba took some of the sindoor and wrote something on the ground in an unfamiliar script, using only the little finger of his right hand. Rinchen told me he was writing 'Amar Trivedi', the name of the subject. Then he stretched out that hand and his assistants placed the clay doll in it. The baba grabbed the doll and flung it into the pyre.

The chanting went on for a quarter of an hour. The little hut was filled with smoke and the rhythmic enunciation of the mantras. My eyes were fixed on the clay doll in the pyre and the skull behind it, which looked strangely animated with the flames dancing around it. It was a bizarre environment, definitely not for the faint-hearted.

Then, abruptly, it stopped, and the babas ceased their chanting. They threw handfuls of sindoor from another box into the pyre. The flames died down. This was another strange thing that I witnessed—I have seen pyres being extinguished with mud or water, but this was the first time I was seeing sindoor being used for the purpose.

Without waiting for the fumes to disperse, the baba thrust his hand into them. As I watched with some trepidation, he brought his hand out and it had the doll in it. The fire had hardened the clay. Mumbling something under his breath, he handed it over to one of his assistants. They put the doll on the floor and then all of them, in some kind of oddly synchronized motion, brought down their open palms on it with great force. The doll crumbled back into mud.

The baba looked at me. He had some kind of a thread in his hand. I realized he was giving it to me. I took it.

'This is no ordinary thread,' he spoke at last. 'It is fortified with the power of our magic. Keep it with you. All you have to do is let the man see this thread. Once he does, within three days, he will return your money.'

I smiled to myself. Without mincing any words, I'd say that everything that they did seemed to be a dramatic show put up for my benefit. There was nothing to come out of this. I had no such friend at all; so what would happen? If these people were real seers, they should have understood that right away. I still decided to play along and put the thread in my pocket.

'What if I never meet my friend again?' I asked.

'Even then, our magic will not go waste,' he said in a booming voice. 'Within a month, one way or the other, you will get your money back.'

I wanted to say something else, but just then another person entered the hut. He was a diminutive man and stood with his hands joined and head bowed with much deference. The baba dismissed me and I left the hut with Rinchen.

We had walked some distance when we heard someone come running behind us. It was the youngest assistant of the baba.

'What happened?' I asked as the assistant tried to regain his breath.

'You wanted to see our ritual?' he said. 'You have a chance this evening. That man who just came . . . his brother is a cripple. He has never walked in his life. If you want, come and see how the baba makes him walk.'

'Really?' I asked. This was something I would not want to miss for anything.

'Yes, but there's a charge.'

'Of course!' I exclaimed. The sarcasm was lost on him. 'How much?'

'For only seeing, 500 rupees.'

I gave him the money and walked away after finding out the details.

———

I had initially intended to stay in the same hut till evening and wait for the ritual to begin, but Rinchen took me away from there with an excuse. He made me wait in another hut where a local offered us tea and some simple snacks. There, my companion told me that the babas don't allow anyone to look at their 'preparations'. However, at the ritual in the evening, there was expected to be a huge crowd. Such healing was a big event in Mayong.

At 5 p.m., we reached the ground where the ritual was to take place. It was behind the hut we were in before. I saw the same baba who had orchestrated the first ritual in the hut, but his assistants were all missing. He was chanting something, while a large crowd of the locals had assembled. I waited with them. Then the baba stood up and started walking. Everyone began to follow him, evidently aware of what was happening. It appeared as if I was the only clueless one there, but I went with the crowd.

The baba took us to another bigger ground. What I saw made my jaw drop. I am being totally honest. I am seldom surprised by things, but the spectacle that presented itself to me here was beyond my wildest imagination.

There was a raging bonfire, much bigger than the one in the hut, and a circle of white powder was drawn on the ground around it. And—here's the shocking part—above the bonfire, on a wooden frame that had been erected, a near-naked man was hung upside-down. He was tied to the frame by his ankles. His arms were tied to his torso to prevent them from dangling down. His head was only about 5–6 feet above the flames. And just beyond the flames, I could see an empty wheelchair.

When I first saw the man, his back was to me, but then his body slowly turned and I could see his face. His eyes were shut, but shockingly, there was a smile on his face. That smile was the most horrifying part of it all.

The chanting was going on in full swing now. The baba was joined by two more and they were furiously spouting syllables, while someone else poured something into the flames. I think it was ghee, which made the flames leap out. Whenever they did that, I skipped a heartbeat as the flames would almost reach up to the man's head.

And the crippled man was still smiling.

I saw four poles erected at the four corners of the bonfire. The poles had human skulls affixed atop them.

A rooster was brought, held by its wings. Its miserable squawking mingled with the chanting, and then it suddenly stopped. I saw the head of the rooster falling right into the flames.

This was too much for me. I wanted to do something, but by now there were about a hundred people there. Their faces were flushed with excitement, with some kind of resolve, as if they were witnessing a miracle of great significance. I could see a frightening amount of devotion on their faces, and when one is surrounded by such belief, the wisest thing to do is stay quiet.

After about half an hour of this inhuman torture inflicted on the man, someone brought a large amount of sindoor and threw it on the fire. The fire died out, and as it crackled, the powder of sindoor dispersed in the air and gave many people a coughing fit.

The man was brought down by two assistants. His hair was singed. His face was practically blackened with the soot.

The two assistants propped him on their shoulders and brought him to his wheelchair. There was a deathly silence now.

The baba walked up to the man, who was now slumped in the wheelchair. He took an oddly shaped stick and beat it on the ground in front of the cripple. It was a means to get him to start walking, but the man did not move. He stayed limp in the chair. The baba tried this for about five minutes and then he let out an angry huff and went back to his assistants.

There was a murmur in the crowd.

Suddenly, a woman started wailing out loud. She was surrounded by a small group of people and I could see the man who had come into the hut in the afternoon. I gathered this was the cripple's family.

'What's going on?' I asked Rinchen.

Rinchen tried to listen. I could see the baba now. He was sitting under a tree and there was fire in his eyes.

'The baba is furious,' said Rinchen.

'Why?'

'The treatment did not work.'

'But why did it not work?'

'The baba says the man's handicap is not a mere physical disability. The man is actually possessed.'

'Possessed? As in spirits?' I did not want to tell him about my work with spirits. Right from the start, I had not sensed any spirits in all of Mayong.

'Yes. That is why the rite did not work. The baba performed the ritual for simple healing, but they needed to do an exorcism.'

Someone near us said something to Rinchen and his eyes grew wide in wonder. I asked him what it was and he said, 'The baba cannot see his resident ghost any more. That's why he is furious. The ghost possessing the cripple was so strong that it killed the baba's resident ghost. Anyway, let's not wait here. The ritual is done. We should head back.'

I walked with him to another car that he had arranged for me to go back. Before getting into the car, I asked him, 'Have you ever seen anyone being healed by these babas?'

'Why, sure! People talk all the time about—'

'No, I am not asking you about what people talk. I am asking you if you have seen something with your own eyes.'

Rinchen fell into deep thought. I knew he would not answer. I got into the car and signalled the driver to start.

———

A hundred thoughts ran through my mind during the ride back to Guwahati. The entire episode in Mayong had only consolidated my firm belief that black magic is nothing but an illusion. When I say that, I mean an illusion like a simple magician's card trick. When we see that, or even when we see a magician on stage pulling a rabbit out of a hat, we know that there is some trick hidden away somewhere. We call it magic because we cannot explain it, but we know there's a logical explanation behind it.

I have always felt that black magic also falls in that domain. I believe that these black magicians are illusionists too, but their secrets are so closely guarded that no one has ever been privy to them. That is probably why they live in obscurity and lead such fearsome lives. It is to drive most people away, while they continue to practise their craft for those who believe all too easily.

Just think about it—India has hundreds of thousands of babas and *tantriks*. If all of these people indeed had magical powers, then why would we all have to struggle so much? Why is there sickness? Why is there death? Why is there an enemy at our nation's borders? Our babas and their curses would have been enough. But the irony is that the babas themselves fall ill, they themselves die. When they don't have control over their own existence, how can they claim to have control over others? This simple logic escapes most of us.

Or maybe we want to believe in babas and tantriks. Maybe it gives us some comfort in knowing that there is a solution to even the most difficult problem in life, however illogical it might seem on the surface. I think that's what it is—the hope of a resolution keeps our superstitions afloat.

Mayong was a truly different experience for me. Though I did not shatter any myths there, the experience opened my eyes to so many things. It made me understand that when it comes to the faith of people, there are few other explanations that will work.

7

A Carnival of Ghosts

CONSIDERING MY FIELD of work, I have had my share of bizarre experiences. They go with the territory. There have been nights when I have ventured into spooky mines, roamed the ramparts of abandoned forts and ghost towns, broken into desolate chapels, and more. And yet, there is one night that stands out for its mélange of outrageous oddities. The night I spent at Sonpur Bhoot Mela, which, as the name suggests, is a 'ghost fair', held annually in a town named Sonpur in Bihar.

In this chilling story, I take you through the many incredible incidents I witnessed at this most unusual fair.

In November 2016, during a slow period between my projects, I took the opportunity to visit my native town in Patna. I was working in Mumbai at the time, but for a young bachelor like me, a trip home also meant saving on expenses as living in the maximum city without any work in hand was not a feasible option.

Inevitably, boredom began to seep in after the first week. Having spent a couple of years in the razzle-dazzle of Mumbai, my quaint little hometown was proving to be lacklustre in comparison. My childhood buddies had all moved to other places around the globe so I didn't have their company either. Now don't get me wrong, Patna is home for me, and I will defend it till my dying breath, but it is also true that the city does not have much to offer to an adrenalin-charged youth with a sense of thrill and adventure like me.

So there I was, fidgeting away, trying to find things to do to keep myself occupied, when I heard that a famed annual cattle fair was under way in the nearby village of Sonpur.

Any self-respecting Patnaite would have heard of the Sonpur Cattle Fair, which is also touted as the world's largest animal exhibition, in which hordes of people from all over the world converge at this lesser-known town. The fair starts on the full moon night of Kartik Poornima in November and runs for a month. During this period, the little hamlet is transformed into a bustling place, receiving a big boost in every aspect of its life—social, moral and, most importantly, commercial.

Long ago, as a child, I had been to the fair with my family. The daylong outing was reduced to vague scraps of disjointed memories—glimpses of many, many animals, and people bartering them for goods and money, and the usual games and foods that are generally seen at such melas. It had been a chaotic but exciting family excursion. The prospect of revisiting it now was exhilarating and evoked a fair degree of nostalgia.

I decided to make the trip alone; I didn't need company for this. Sonpur is an easily manageable hour's drive from Patna, and you can feel the hubbub all along the route as you travel. I picked a weekday morning, loaded my cameras into my car and set out on the journey. My intention was to capture as many candid moments at the fair as possible. Maybe I could blog about it later, or simply add the pictures to my private collection.

It was nearing noon when I reached Sonpur. I stepped out of my car with great eagerness, but I didn't realize that I was heading for a huge anticlimax.

No sooner did I enter the ground than I felt all my warm fuzzy feelings turn to dust. The memories stored in my mind as a child could not be more different from the visuals I now beheld in front of me. The vast sea of animals was still there—herds of cows and buffalos, horses and deer, dogs and cats of all possible breeds, and even elephants—and the buying and selling was being conducted as always in raucous voices. But there ended the resemblance. Everything else had undergone a dramatic makeover. The carnival was modernized, far more organized, with stalls and sheds lined up for better showing and viewing, and stalls of food and drink and toys, including a recreation area for kids. To my mind, it appeared as if the people were speaking in a more refined tongue too—more businesslike as opposed to the crude banter that was the backbone of the fair back in those days. The bucolic feel and raw energy had all been vitiated by this new swankiness that seemed to come from a different world.

But I was here now, and I wanted to make the most of it.

I brought out my DSLR camera and started scouting around to catch animals and people in moments of candid glee. Fortunately, there was no dearth of those, for, unlike me, the visitors were absolutely in their element. I was the lone crusader trying to scratch beneath the layers to unearth a past reserve of memories. But there was a joyful vivacity in the throng, complemented well by the vibrancy of the colours of their apparel. I captured many a vivid scene, of old men and women, of boisterous families with their numerous children, of the children by themselves at the toy stalls, and, of course, of the many animals that were being bartered.

And then my camera focused on a slender, dark-complexioned man, probably in his early twenties, running back and forth with a great deal of worry lining his face.

Perhaps he sensed that my camera was pointed at him, and he came up to me.

'Hey,' he spoke in a rush, 'have you seen a woman in an orange sari with a red border? Wheatish-complexioned? She is about this tall.'

I shook my head. 'Who is she?' I asked.

'My wife,' he said quickly. 'I went to get some cold drinks and she just disappeared.'

'Oh! You want me to help you look for her?'

He was so flustered that he did not even recognize my offer of help and cursorily nodded a yes.

I tagged along with Puran (that was the name he gave me later) to look for his wife. He described her some more as we scoured the place and showed me her picture on his cell phone, but it was a daunting task. On that day, I think there were close to 10,000 people at the carnival, besides the animals. There was constant movement all around. To add to the complication, every second person was dressed in some shade of orange.

After running around in circles for a considerable amount of time, we came up to an old man, a bangle seller. He took one long look at the photograph and, with a long drag on his smoking pipe, said, 'Go home.'

The words were like a slap to Puran.

'Why do you say that, *kaka*?' I asked.

'Won't find her!' he said in a voice that sounded much more ominous in his Bihari-accented Hindi—'*Nahin milegi* [Won't find her]!'

Those two words and the way they had been said made Puran's legs wobble. I steadied him and made him sit on the embankment next to the old man, before I asked, 'Why do you say that?'

The old man looked skywards as if he were expecting to see something in the clouds. 'That is what happens to young women who are left alone here.'

'What happens?'

'They are taken away.'

'By whom?'

To that, he did not reply.

I insisted, 'Kaka, please help this man. He looks like he will have a heart attack now. If you know anything, please tell me.'

'Come back at night,' said the old man after another long pause. 'But don't come here. Go there'—he pointed—'there's a maidan about a kilometre ahead.'

'What happens there?'

He leaned forward, so close that I could clearly see the cataracts in his eyes, and said two words that set my pulse racing.

'Bhoot Mela.'

I volunteered to look for Puran's wife and we scanned every inch of the place. We had announcements made and spoke to the police guards on duty, but there was no trace of her. Puran told me that their marriage was just three months old, that she was from Kanpur and knew nothing about this place. There was nowhere she could have gone, and no reason for her to go anywhere of her own volition.

The words that were ringing in my mind were *Bhoot Mela*. What could a 'ghost fair' really mean? Would there be ghosts dancing around? Spirits materializing out of thin air and putting on a show? I kicked myself for not having my work equipment with me, but this was certainly something I would not want to miss. And—the more intriguing bit—how could a ghost fair that was held annually, practically in my own backyard, have escaped my attention all these years?

After that portentous proclamation from the old bangle-seller, I probed around further and gathered some information from the regulars at the fair, the stall owners and animal sellers. What I learned was the kind of stuff an exotic documentary on Indian occult practices would be made of.

The Bhoot Mela kicks off every year on the night of Kartik Poornima on an open ground situated close (but also hidden) from the main venue of the cattle fair. There is no parking there and people have to reach it by foot. People of all faiths come here with various intentions, but mostly to rid themselves of ghostly possessions or to win some occult powers. The fair is run by faith healers, clairvoyants, mediums, diviners, seers, practitioners of the dark arts and their ilk; you find all sorts of them here. These *tantriks* and *ojha*s set up their stalls on the ground itself, and their wares include charms and chants, potions and talismans and a myriad of stuff that offer the various things that seekers come looking for. You could either buy stuff from them, or you could 'rent' it for a period of time. This even applied to chants, such as mantra protections.

I was fascinated to learn that these babas could give you a chant that would work for you for a week or a month or six months, depending on how much you paid for it! And once you are done with it, you could also 'sell' the mantra protection to someone else! Wonders never cease, do they?

But I wanted inside information. No one was really willing to talk much. Were these really ghosts here? Or was this just a freak show with a theme? People alluded to the fact that this is the night when all ghosts come down to earth and visit the ground, and that the most hair-raising things happen in full view of the numerous visitors. Some people shared with me accounts of levitation and telekinesis and even some paranormal activity. Ghosts? But why would they decide to have a carnival of this kind, that too in such a mob-like presence of humans? What was this unearthly show anyway?

One person—a keychain seller—told us that we should not visit the mela at all. He said, in no mean words, 'Sahib, don't go there. It isn't a place for the likes of you. If you don't have belief, your lives could be destroyed. Bhoot Mela is not just a carnival; it is a place where really dark things happen.'

None of those words deterred me, of course!

I told Puran that we'd find his wife if she was at the mela, and he thanked me profusely for my assistance. I was glad I could do something benevolent for a fellow human being even while pursuing something that held my complete interest.

———

When dusk approached, I offered Puran something to eat (which he refused) and led him to the venue of the Bhoot Mela. He was distraught but hadn't lost hope yet, perhaps sustained by my company. But I could see that he was still in a fragile state, and I didn't know if I should give him any hope either. There was also another challenge for him. He was a layperson with no experience of the occult whatsoever; on the contrary, the very mention of 'Bhoot Mela' had roused much fear in him. For him to visit or even think about such a place was a very big deal, but I could see that he had steeled himself on account of his wife. It was some true love that I was witnessing there. Love can make you brave like nothing else can.

Leaving my vehicle parked safely at the cattle-fair ground, I walked up to the maidan in question with Puran in tow. The full moon's light guided our steps. The cattle fair was behind us and activities seemed to have completely stilled there, but soon we began to hear a different kind of commotion up ahead. Puran and I exchanged looks. We were on the right track. There was indeed something going on in the maidan that had been silent all through the day.

And there it was.

The open ground was teeming with people—people of all shapes and sizes. To me, it felt as though the commotion was akin to that found during the daytime at the cattle fair, perhaps even more so. While there we had found some semblance of organization, here everything was much more chaotic.

Fascinated, I walked on. It was indeed as described. All sorts of tantriks, ojhas, maulanas and suchlike had set up shop on the grounds. They had with them various articles of their practice—feathers, charms, old yellowing tomes, vials filled with various dubious potions and the bones of animals, birds and even humans. They wore the garb characteristic of their kind—long gowns of red or black and huge colourful turbans and many-beaded necklaces. With their faces smeared with powders of many hues and their eyes a burning amber, perhaps on account of these powders swirling in the air, these babas seemed wholly absorbed in their chanting and swaying and dancing. And surrounding each of them, a group of people stood and watched, tantalized, as they received services from the babas in ways that could raise a thousand questions.

I could not deny that such a place would be fertile ground for any kind of paranormal investigation—as would any place that claimed to be the convergence point of all kinds of ethereal entities, conjured up by the devices of a legion that dabbled in the dark arts. Once again regretting not bringing along any of my devices, I took out my camera and started clicking a few pictures to freeze these fringe oddities of our culture.

'What state will I find my wife in? What must have happened to her?' Puran said, reminding me of his presence.

The terror in his eyes was palpable. His words took away my fascination for everything around and reminded me of our main quest.

So far, we had been standing at the periphery of the venue and observing things from outside. The time had come to take the plunge and get into the thick of things. I made a sign to Puran to follow and we strode in, amid the reciting and dancing, checking out every stall for any hint of the missing woman.

It was a display of manic proportions.

At one stall, an elderly man sat seeking a cure for his impotence. At another, a woman was praying for release from domestic abuse. At yet another, a group of young men were asking about their professional growth. Further along, we saw sick people getting 'treated'. The gullibility of the human race was on full parade here, and as I walked deeper into the melee, I found things getting increasingly curious. At one of the stalls, a woman with one glass eye was reading people's futures with cards picked up by a parrot, and there was a queue of seekers at her stall. There was another where a young woman was being beaten with a broom by a tantrik. I thought of intervening and stopping him, but I was told that the woman was possessed by a vengeful spirit and they had come to this mela specifically for this kind of exorcism.

The more I saw, the more I realized the appalling nature of these goings-on. I had great expectations from this place, but now I could see the sham that it was. Ghosts don't converge at a place like this for a party. They don't possess you in this manner. Even if they do, thrashing the one possessed with a broom and reciting random mantras don't get them out. The young woman was close to being molested at the hands of that tantrik, and my bigger worry was that this seemed to be a socially sanctioned practice.

I didn't have my equipment that day, but I didn't need it to tell me that all of this was just a big farce put up for credulous people.

I sensed Puran shuddering at these sights. We were now at the very heart of the Bhoot Mela and were encountering the more vicious, more malevolent practices running riot in the place. When I saw a baba poking needles into the bare back of a man and actually letting his blood out, I thought I had seen it all, but something more sinister was lying in wait.

A huge flurry at the far end of the maidan stopped us in our tracks. Following something that I could not quite discern yet, I saw tons of men and women making a mad rush in that direction. We barely stepped aside and saved ourselves from getting trampled underfoot. They were shouting something as they ran, and for a while I could not understand what it was.

And then I did. These were horrifying cries of, '*Daayan! Daayan!*' which meant, 'Witch! Witch!' It brought a knot to my chest.

Witch.

If there is one word that has never boded well for women in India since ancient times, this is it. In those days of patriarchy, women were singled out at the slightest pretext and branded as witches. But these were spiteful acts of vengeance; vengeance unleashed by men because the women had spoken out against male dominance, or were simply perceived to be threatening to their unfair customs on account of the clothes they wore, the language they spoke, or the professions they chose. The ultimate fate of these unfortunate women would be in the hands of the men who ran the societies, who would have no qualms whatsoever in lynching the women or burning them at the stake, after abusing them in unmentionable ways and then discarding them by the roadside.

There are alarming statistics on witches. One figure claims that, throughout history, around 2100 women have been murdered in India after being labelled as witches. Today, the Indian government has outlawed practices such as witchcraft, which means people cannot resort to calling women by this epithet any more, but like all other banned practices, it still prevails in far-flung and nondescript parts of the country.

And here it was so brazenly displayed out in the open. Not just that, the entire event was well attended, and it was held every year!

My nerves prickling with the anticipation of what I might find, I proceeded with cautious steps. The crowd was looking in one direction and that made it easy for me to know where I should head. I made my way through the onlookers and stumbled upon a sight that made my blood freeze.

A middle-aged woman was sitting on the ground, her hair loose, her eyelids fluttering, her lips quivering. A large swathe of red powder was smeared across her forehead. Thick beads of perspiration shone on her body even on that chilly night as if she were in a furnace, and they made her dark skin glisten. She sat cross-legged, feet tucked under her, hands on her knees, and was in some kind of trance that did not look humanly at all.

'What is wrong with her?' I asked a man in the crowd.

'She is a daayan!' he said and promptly bid me to keep mum, not wanting to lose one glimpse of the spectacle.

A tantrik made his appearance from the middle of the crowd. Nearly six-and-a-half-feet tall, his hair matted into dreadlocks and a blazing mark of some austerity on his forehead, he presented a fearsome sight. The moment he showed up, the crowd fell into a hush, making it clear that this was the man who would run things from here onwards.

And he did.

He came and stood near the woman, towering over her, and asked a question in the deepest voice I have ever heard.

'Speak, woman, are you a daayan?'

The woman did not say anything. Instead, she began to slowly murmur something and her head made a weird sort of nodding circular motion. The crowd gasped. Adults shoved their children behind them and continued watching the scene themselves, their faces a picture of terror.

The tantrik took centre stage. He cast a sweeping glance around the assembled people and said in a sonorous voice, 'This woman is indeed a witch. A daayan. She cannot be allowed to go back like this. The purification has to happen.'

A slender wraith-like man, his teeth chattering in the cold, asked, 'What will the purification be, baba?'

'Are you the husband?' the tantrik asked.

The man nodded.

'Your wife is on the path of grave sin!' the tantrik roared. 'She will thrash and flail and it will be a spectacle to strike terror in everyone's hearts, but you have to hold her steady. You hear me?'

The husband's body began to shake and tremble, but he nodded.

'Go on and hold her. I will purify her now. I will lie on top of her and quash the evil that is within her. Go!'

I was so stunned by it all that a stroke of inaction gripped me in its vice. I should have done something right then, but the crowd was large and in a state of frenzy. I just walked away. They numbered in the hundreds and were manic, with brainwashed minds; what could I have done to change things there? I seek some comfort in the fact that at least I didn't stand by to watch that shameful scene. I did not witness any further what happened to that poor woman, but I am sure that whatever happened gave those onlookers a perverse amount of voyeuristic delight. There were hoots and catcalls and I could hear the tantrik chanting above all, syllables that were interspersed with the most vulgar moans I have ever heard.

Amidst the mayhem, I felt Puran tugging at my hand. Honestly, I had even forgotten that he was there with me, but his plea brought me back. '*Bhaiya*, where is my wife?' he asked. Tears were swimming in his eyes now. The acts that had unfolded before them were considered worse than death in his society. I could understand the turmoil that his mind must have been in and I decided to go out once again and look for her.

And then, just like that, I found her.

———

She was there, looking exactly as she did in the picture on her husband's phone, sitting in the manner of someone awaiting death.

Dressed in the attire that her husband had described, looking lost and forlorn, she sat dazed with a group of seven or eight other women of about the same age as her. They were all newly married too; the marks of their recent weddings were still upon them. Like her, they were all sitting on the ground, a little away from the crowd, completely unaware of what was going on just a few steps away from where they were.

The moment Puran saw her, despite all my cautioning, he went up to her screaming and running.

'Tulsi! Tulsi! Where have you been?' he yelled.

His wife turned to look at him, but for a long frightening moment, there was no sign of recognition in her eyes at all. Something horrible had been done to her. Puran didn't hold back though. He grabbed her by the hand and shook it.

Something snapped in her, like the vestiges of a stupor.

'Wh-what . . . where am I?' she stuttered.

'You don't know? Where were you?' Puran asked, wildly gesticulating in his despair.

The story tumbled out in fits and bursts. She said that a man had approached her at the cattle fair in the morning and he had given her something that looked like a ticket. He had said it was a free lottery ticket. It had a funny smell, like a blend of garlic and cinnamon, and she meant to say as much to the person who gave her the ticket, but when she looked up to see him, everything seemed to be whirling around.

The next moment, she felt faint. She remembered going weak-kneed and then collapsing. But she didn't hit the ground. Something—or someone—had held her. She remembered falling into those hairy arms, but remembered nothing afterwards.

'What the—' Puran began, struggling for words.

I saw the urgency of the situation. For whatever reason, these women had been abducted. Perhaps they were the next in line to be a part of that evil ritual that was going on in the circle ahead. I had heard of tantriks performing bizarre sex rituals to gain powers or simply to satisfy their lust, and to that end, they'd have no qualms in publicly decreeing those poor women to be witches. Surely this one had someone he worked in collaboration with, an associate who tricked and stupefied women and brought them to him. In no mean words, I told Puran that he should take his wife and get out of there as soon as possible and never come back to this wretched place.

Puran did just that. He thanked me multiple times and took his still-dazed wife with him.

I was left standing there alone now, at the farthest end of the Bhoot Mela, and there were more women in front of me in need of rescuing. I did not know the best way to do it though, and while I was weighing my options, I saw a police constable. I ran to him as fast as my legs could carry me and told him about what was happening. His face changed colour. Shouting out an expletive, he said, 'These people are not meant to do this here!' Raising his lathi, he rushed in the direction of where the insane ritual was being performed.

Relieved, I left the place a moment later.

———

There are no words to describe how odd that entire night had been. I was right in the midst of what was an accepted arena for all things supernatural. Ghosts and spirits and other paranormal things were being spoken about as though they were a part of the normal world. People don't accept such things easily in the daytime and they don't discuss them with familiar people, but when you bring them under the cloak of darkness and anonymity, their true colours begin to show.

I saw some of the most unbelievable acts that humans are capable of indulging in. It was a haven for all kinds of illicit activities to go on, almost unchecked. But what shocked me to the core was that I saw, for the first time, such a wide acceptance for such activities, all of which were being carried out shamelessly in the name of faith.

To answer the bigger question, did I see any ghosts that day? Real ghosts, I mean. No, I didn't see any. I had been dabbling in the paranormal for a while before I went to Sonpur, and that had given me an innate sense of being able to tell if there is something 'otherworldly' in anything I witness. It's just a knack that I have developed over time. That night, I saw all the worst manifestations of humans, but only humans. I didn't perceive any *bhoot* at the Bhoot Mela.

People will believe what they want to believe. And such is the case at the Bhoot Mela too.

All was definitely not lost though. Years have passed, but even today I think of Puran and the big teary-eyed smile he blessed me with when I reunited him with his wife.

8

The Royal Spirits of the
Three Kings Chapel

BEACHES, CASINOS, CRUISES—Goa offers adventurous activities aplenty amid nature's bounty in vast measure, deservedly making it the most popular travel destination of the country. But a lesser-known fact is that Goa has more than its fair share of haunted locations.

The Three Kings Chapel, also known as Our Lady of Remedios Chapel, is counted among these. Situated on Cuelim Hill in the village of Cansaulim, this small but beautiful chapel has been a hotspot for paranormal enthusiasts. Though the chapel authorities and locals are quite against the idea of there being anything out of the ordinary about the place, it continues to attract significant attention in my fraternity.

This is the story of a young couple I met who had had a terrifying experience while touring the chapel and then embarked on a journey to rid themselves of the 'problem' they seemed to have brought back home with them.

It was a slightly chilly mid-December night in Mumbai's suburb of Bandra. I had just wound up a talk on paranormal experiences at a Café Coffee Day outlet, bid the guests goodbye and was relaxing with a cappuccino. The warmth of the coffee gave my throat some much-needed comfort after the longish, fairly animated talk. I was immersed in its flavours when I noticed a young couple staring at me from the table across. I noticed that there was nothing on their table and they were talking in whispers while looking in my direction. I held my gaze, and they saw I had noticed that they were watching me. That made them visibly embarrassed. After a brief moment of hushed consultation with each other, they came up to my table with half-smiles.

The man spoke first. 'Hello, Jay sir. We were at the talk you just gave. We heard every word.'

'Thanks!' I said, smiling back at them.

There was an awkward silence again, during which I saw the woman jab her elbow into the man's side. Then he spoke again, 'Sir, my name is Vikas and this is Sunidhi. We are . . . a couple. We live in Bandra.'

'All right,' I said, still smiling.

I sensed the man's confusion. He clearly wanted to say more, and I wanted him to take his time. I could see he was still trying to decide whether to tell me or not. He looked the nervous kind, going by appearance. He had a short crop of curly hair that made him look much younger than he was, and he wore thick, black-rimmed glasses that sat so perfectly on his nose, one would think he was born with them. I could see a small bead of sweat beginning to trickle down the side of his head.

'Would you like to sit down?' I asked.

'Sure!' said the woman and immediately pulled up a chair. She sat down long before her companion did.

'Okay, so what do you want to talk about?' I decided to be direct.

'Jay, I hope you can spare us a few minutes,' said the woman. 'We are in a bit of a mess, and maybe only you can help us out.'

'Sure,' I said. 'Go on, I am listening.'

She hesitated for a moment before launching into her story.

'Something is happening in our house. There is no explanation for it. But it has to do with something paranormal. That's why we came to you.'

At least she did not beat around the bush. She didn't look the type either. With her straight hair, no-nonsense expression and eloquent manner of speaking, she looked like someone who handled communications at a corporate office. She leaned forward as she spoke, a clear sign that she was taking the lead in this conversation now.

'Tell me about your experience, Sunidhi.' I deliberately said her name to make her feel comfortable and safe. 'I'm always up for a good story.'

'Only that this isn't a story, if you don't mind,' she said quickly. 'This thing has made our life hell.'

She smiled as she said that, but that smile had no mirth in it. I noticed the dark circles under her eyes. Not a good sign at all for her age. She must have been in her early twenties at the most.

'Let's start then,' I said.

'So it is about this time we went to Goa last year . . .'

'Oh! Goa, did you say?'

'Yes.'

'Interesting. I am leaving for Goa in three days too.'

She nodded.

'Go on, tell me what's bothering you. Will you have some coffee as you talk?'

And here's how their story rolled out.

———

Almost a year ago, in December 2016, Vikas and Sunidhi were in Goa. They were a young urban couple, living together with no strings attached. Goa had been a spur-of-the-moment decision, more of a road trip than anything else. Avoiding all the touristy traps of North Goa, they decided to put up in the relatively quieter Madgaon in South Goa. It was an idyllic vacation, as peaceful as could be, as they bike-hopped from one spectacular destination to another in the hinterland. Then they heard about the Three Kings Chapel in Cansaulim.

A hotel guide told them intriguing things about the place. The chapel dates back to the sixteenth century. It is a beautiful Portuguese structure, tucked away in one of the much-forgotten parts of Goa. Tourists rarely visit this off-beat spot. However, the chapel is a thriving hub of activity in Cansaulim on 6 January every year, when the Feast of the Three Kings is celebrated. During this feast, three teenaged boys are dressed as kings and led in a colourful procession to the chapel, where the festivities last the entire day. But otherwise the chapel is quiet almost all year round. Mass services are conducted in silence with only small groups of people, so much so that the area has acquired a quaint and mysterious air about it over the centuries.

When the hotel guide described the serene and beautiful chapel and called it a must-visit attraction, the young couple were keen on a visit. An outing was duly planned for the next afternoon itself. The couple started from Madgaon on their motorbike, weaving through several confusing roads and asking directions from locals since map apps did not show the shortest routes, or even the correct routes, in most cases.

It was nearing evening when they reached the chapel. When they saw it, they wondered why they had had so much difficulty in locating it, for it is a large white edifice with an imposing facade. It has a triangular head with a white cross at the top. The entire structure is painted a pristine white, and the colour has, surprisingly, stayed unblemished over the ages. The windows and the main gate have red awnings over them. And given that it is located on a hill—Cuelim Hill— the tall white chapel shines like a beacon.

Standing in the proximity of the imposing structure, the couple felt elevated. There was this aura that they felt, the strange lightness of being that all religious places make one feel, no matter how many centuries old they are. It made them clasp each other's hands and smile and, overcome by peace, they walked in.

Whatever they had heard about the place did not do justice to how beautiful it really was. As they came up to the chapel, they discovered that it provided a breathtaking view of the landscape. Standing on the hilltop, they could see the entire village for miles around. Wherever they looked, they saw verdant greens and deep-red soil, and the breeze that blew in from the nearby sea put them in a different mood altogether.

Once inside, the area wasn't big, but it certainly compensated for that with its splendour. There were little charming details everywhere, most notably the altar. A spiral staircase that led to an upper floor had a distinctive personality of its own. The couple stood in awe for long, deeply moved, feeling a strong sense of reverence, soaking in the silence of the chapel.

Vikas and Sunidhi didn't realize how they passed two hours in this wondrous place. Basking in its tranquillity, both inside and out, they were even oblivious to the few other people who had come to visit. They didn't say much, just sat hand in hand and contemplated on the unique kind of peace that these confines offered.

But as the sun began to set, the bliss was broken.

A man materialized almost out of nowhere and began urging all visitors in a polite but firm voice to leave the place. The couple took him to be a chapel security official. He came up to Vikas and Sunidhi as well.

The couple did not wish to leave the serene atmosphere so early in the evening though, and requested whether they could wait a little longer. But the man was quite adamant, insisting that the chapel needed to be locked and that the premises weren't safe as they might be visited by stray dogs.

Heaving a sigh of despair, the couple walked out, even as the man produced a large lock and shut the heavy arched doorway with an audible bang.

Now, Vikas and Sunidhi had only gone up to their bike when the sun set completely, and the sole light in the entire place was the moonlight that was just beginning to intensify. They stood for a few minutes in the silence of the night when Sunidhi suddenly proposed that they should go to the chapel again. 'We have come from so far; let's spend some more time in there,' she told her companion.

Vikas was outraged by the suggestion at first, but eventually gave in.

'It is an adventure,' Sunidhi convinced him. 'And just imagine! An entire building as beautiful as that and just the two of us inside.'

Vikas bought into the plan. They were a young couple, very much in love, and youth lent them that particular shade of recklessness that is a hallmark of that age. So back into the chapel they walked, this time more excited than before but also making sure that nobody was watching them as they tried to find a way in.

Sunidhi almost squealed aloud in delight when she found a window that hadn't been bolted from the inside. With a twinkle of mischief in her eyes, she clambered in first and then helped Vikas in as well.

She led him to the last pew and they sat there, hand in hand, as they had been earlier.

The chapel looked different now. In just a matter of minutes, it had been plunged into darkness and the only light was the blue-tinted moonlight filtering in through the windows. They sat and stared as this light danced in the eyes of the various statues of saints lining the walls, giving them a lifelike quality.

'Don't these statues look creepy in the night?' Sunidhi remarked, going up to one of them.

'Shh!' Vikas admonished her lightly. 'Don't say that about holy people. You might be cursed.'

Sunidhi backed off and touched her ears. 'Sorry!' she mumbled.

They walked around the place, talking, giggling, standing close to each other, taking in each and every minute detail.

And so the foolhardy young couple decided to spend the night in the 400-year-old chapel, doing things that bordered on mischief but also afraid to malign the sanctity of the place. Their only whim was an innocent wish to stay there till morning dawned.

Little did they realize what they had gotten themselves into.

It was around 11.30 p.m. when they began to feel slightly drowsy. And then a particular incident occurred that they wouldn't forget for the rest of their lives.

They were sitting at two ends of a pew, cross-legged, facing each other, talking in order to stay awake. Vikas was narrating a story from a college picnic that he had gone on long ago, when the air suddenly went cold. A distinct smell suffused the air, the smell of something burning. Vikas froze mid-sentence and looked at Sunidhi with an expression of the greatest fear.

'What is it?' she asked, the darkness not allowing her to see his expression clearly right away.

But Vikas was dumbfounded. He raised a finger and pointed at her.

'What is it?'

'Don't . . . turn!' he said in a feeble voice.

Immediately, Sunidhi felt a shiver run down her spine.

'You are scaring me, Vikas,' she whispered. 'Stop your prank.'

'Don't look back . . .'

'Why? What's there?'

'I . . . I see . . .'

And he stopped talking abruptly. He couldn't voice it, at least not at that moment. But he *did* see it. Standing right behind Sunidhi was a tall hooded figure with arms folded— hovering about a foot in the air.

He wanted to tell her to slowly get off the pew. This had been a bad idea. A very bad idea indeed. And even as Vikas kept looking, under its hood, the figure's lips curled into a creepy smile.

'S-Sunidhi . . . we must . . .'

He reached out to touch Sunidhi's arm, and recoiled instantly, withdrawing his hand in utter shock. Sunidhi's arm was stone cold.

Then he looked at her face.

There was an expression of fear written all over it that he hadn't seen before.

'W-what is it, Sunidhi?' he managed.

This time, she raised her finger.

'Behind you,' she said in a voice that seemed to come from the depths of her parched throat. 'There's someone . . . standing . . .'

Vikas felt as if his heart had fallen into his stomach.

'Is it a dark, shadowy, tall figure with its arms folded?'

Sunidhi nodded perfunctorily. Words failed her.

'But I see that same figure behind you too!'

At once, both turned to look behind them.

And they found themselves staring into vacant darkness. The figures had vanished.

Just like that, a candle lit up on the prayer shelf, the flame an upright yellow glow. And there was something about it— despite all the wind in the chapel, the flame did not once flicker.

The petrified couple sprang off the pew, not caring if they fell or hit something. They made a mad scramble to reach the window they had come in through.

Fortunately, the window was still open. Vikas let Sunidhi go out first, and as he tried to climb out, he saw her staring back into the chapel with that same scorched look of fear in her eyes again.

'What . . . what is it?' he asked, now safely outside with her.

'Let's just get out of here as soon as we can, Vikas.'

They ran all the way to where their bike was parked, hopped on and drove away as speedily as they could.

It was about a mile later when she had managed to catch her breath that Sunidhi spoke.

'There was a third figure at the altar, Vikas. I saw it. He was very large, larger than the one I saw behind you, and he was sitting cross-legged on the altar. But actually . . . he wasn't really sitting. He was floating. Floating in the air. And . . . and . . . he was moving towards you. Oh, dear God!'

———

'And we got out of Goa the next day itself, though we had planned to stay for a week,' Sunidhi ended her tale.

Their coffees had long gone cold, untouched.

I sighed. I felt a certain amount of indignation at their foolhardiness. There was also the undeniable fact that these people had violated the norms of a religious shrine.

'But . . . but the story didn't end there,' said Vikas, peering at me unblinkingly through his thick glasses.

'What do you mean?'

He looked at Sunidhi once before continuing.

'We believe that something came back with us that night. And it has been with us ever since.'

I leaned forward. 'What is this *something*?'

'We don't know. But it's there in the house. When we are alone, we can hear it. Footsteps. Someone banging on the door, and when we go to open it, nothing. Just cold wind. Sometimes, a foul stink in the bathroom right in the middle of a fragrant bath.'

'And last month,' Sunidhi piped in, 'I found burned papers in our wastepaper bin. But I am very sure we did not burn anything that day.'

'That's not all,' Vikas took over again. They were talking more loosely now, details tumbling out one after the other.

'This thing, whatever it is, has taken away the happiness of the house. Things aren't going right. My big project did not materialize. Sunidhi fell and broke her leg and was on bed rest for three weeks. We are constantly arguing with each other now, something we never did earlier.'

'We believe, Jay, that all of this is caused by that spirit or whatever it is,' Sunidhi finished. 'Would you please, please come to our house and take a look?'

My interest was aroused, I admit. If there was even an ounce of truth in what these two were saying, I could probably learn something.

'All right, I will come and take a look.'

———

Their house turned out to be just round the block, near the Mount Mary Church steps. On the way, Vikas told me how difficult it was to get a rental house in Bandra for an unmarried couple like them, and they had got this place only because they had agreed to pay a year's rent in advance, which was not refundable. They'd have vacated, but that would mean forfeiting the rent.

We came to the apartment. It was like most Bandra apartments, a cosy two-bedroom–hall–kitchen flat in an old building. The building had no security guard; instead, we were welcomed by a family of cats who meowed angrily as we entered. Their house was on the third floor and there was no elevator. The staircase had age-old yellow lights that made our shadows dance along the walls as we climbed.

Sunidhi opened the door and stepped aside. While Vikas fumbled for the light switch, I entered the house, walked four paces and stopped.

'Don't switch on the lights,' I said softly.

I felt Vikas backing away. He went outside and stood beside Sunidhi in the lobby. I could feel their eyes scrutinizing my every move.

It was there, yes. I could feel it. The moment I walked in through the door, I felt a cold wave rushing across my neck and an intense sorrowful feeling consumed me at once. It felt like being plunged into depression, and this great sense of purposelessness swept over me. I could not say whether the couple could see any physical changes in me from where they stood, but I could feel every strand of hair on my body standing on end.

'What is it?' Sunidhi asked.

I turned to face them, trying not to let any emotion show on my face. They still had to stay in this house. 'You can switch on the lights,' I said.

Five minutes later, we were sitting on a couch in the hall. The lights were on, and I had gulped down two glasses of cold water.

'Spirits are the kings of darkness,' I began. 'Darkness is natural; our lights are artificial. When it is dark, they come out and play. That's why I prevented you from switching on the lights when we entered. I wanted to sense the house in the darkness first.'

'Did you sense anything?' Vikas asked.

'I did,' I said simply. An uneasy silence followed. Sunidhi shifted on the couch, sitting closer to Vikas.

'What?' she asked fearfully.

'I will be upfront,' I said carefully. 'As I walked in, I felt all my emotions draining out. I was filled with negative energy. It seems like your surmise was right.'

Then I saw something out of the corner of my eye. There was a big damp patch on the wall behind them. I stood up and went closer to investigate.

'Why is this area wet?' I asked, looking around. There was no scope for leakage, and it was not the rainy season anyway.

'We never gave that a thought,' said Vikas, and then looked at Sunidhi sharply. 'Come to think of it, didn't that patch appear after we returned from Goa last year?'

Disgruntled spirits often leave their marks in some way or the other. These marks are the places where they emerge from, the mouth of their activities, so to say.

'Listen,' I said, now pulling closer to them. 'I strongly feel that there is something serious going on here. It's a good thing that you asked me to visit.'

'Are we in danger?' Sunidhi asked.

'If they haven't harmed you so far, then that's probably not their intention,' I said. 'But just to be safe, sleep with the lights on.'

'No, but what about us now?' Vikas said, getting off the couch now. 'You say there's an entity in our house. How do we live with that? Can you not do some kind of puja or something?'

I said, as coolly as possible, 'I am not a *tantrik*. I don't know any pujas.'

'But . . . there must be something . . . We cannot leave this house. We have no money to move.'

I walked around the room a bit. My brain cells were working furiously, yet it was difficult. The vibes the house gave me were not conducive to thinking. And that made it all so much worse. This young couple in front of me had crossed a line, but they had paid enough. A year of misery for a night's transgression is too harsh. But what could I do to put them out of that misery?

'Okay,' I said, sitting down again. 'There might be one thing.'

'What?' they asked in unison, their eyes lighting up.

'The spirit latched on to you at the Three Kings Chapel . . .'

'Yes.'

'What usually happens in such scenarios is that if the vessel, which is what you are, goes back to the place of origin, the spirit unlatches itself from the vessel and goes back to the source.'

That sentence came out somewhat haphazardly, but it was the best way I could convey my idea at that point.

It was Sunidhi who broke the silence that followed my pronouncement. 'So, you mean to say we should go back to Three Kings?'

I nodded. 'It might just work.'

'You don't know for sure?'

'No one knows anything about the paranormal for sure.'

Since I already had plans to visit Goa, I wouldn't actually be going out of the way to help them. And in any case, after witnessing all this, how could I not visit the Three Kings Chapel?

Fifteen minutes later, they were booking two tickets to Goa on the same flight as mine.

———

I spent a long day doing as much research as I could on the Three Kings Chapel. I read through all possible material on the Internet and hit the local library. I reached out to my network of fellow paranormal enthusiasts as well. Many of them had already visited the chapel and had different experiences to share. Some vouched for a sinister presence there, while others did not want to talk much about it. However, one guy categorically voiced his opinion that there was nothing spooky about the place and I'd be wasting my time. This person was so vociferous in dissuading me that it actually further strengthened my resolve to visit the place

The following morning, an investigator friend of mine gave me the contact details of a certain Jose Carvalho, a local of Cansaulim. I called Jose right away. He turned out to be an affable chap and, more importantly, he was quite forthcoming with information.

'A lot of people have this misconception that the Three Kings Chapel is named after the three wise kings of the East who came to see Baby Jesus, as it is mentioned in the New Testament,' Jose said. 'This is also because the 6th January festival is on the day of Epiphany, which is the day the world celebrates as the day when the three kings reached the manger in Bethlehem where Jesus was born. But the fact is that our three kings are not those three kings from the Bible.'

That was unexpected information. I kept silent and he continued. 'Many years ago, Cansaulim was home to three Portuguese kings. The oldest of these was Holger Alvunger, who was also the most ambitious of the three. But these men were kings only in name. Portugal had adopted a democratic policy and there was no place for monarchs. Yet these three continued to live in this very same place, which was a palace then, still believing that they were royalty.

'Then one day, Holger called his brothers to dine together. But this was to be their last dinner together. Holger had very craftily instructed the chef to poison the meal. His brothers died a merciless death at the dining table itself. This meal would later be called Cansaulim's very own Last Supper.

'Now, the people of Cansaulim had a soft corner for the younger brothers. When they came to know that Holger had killed them, they surrounded the palace. They were a furious mob, armed with weapons and burning torches. Knowing that there was nothing else he could do, Holger chose to poison himself as well.

'In this way, all three brothers died on the same night in the palace, and none of them could ever become kings, although they lived with the title throughout their lives. The villagers buried them in the hall itself. Later, the palace was converted into a chapel, which is what you see now. In time, the chapel was marred with reports of frightful sightings. People claimed to have seen the spirits of the brothers who, as it appeared, had never left the hall. And so, the legend of the Three Kings Chapel took birth.'

When José finished narrating, I was quiet for a long while, trying to digest this fascinating local legend, marvelling at how well it fit in with the experiences of Vikas and Sunidhi. I thanked José and asked him if there was anyone I should speak to before leaving, anyone I probably needed to seek permission from to carry out an investigation of the place. With a fair amount of reluctance, he gave me the number of one Father Francis, who looked after the management of the chapel. He cautioned me to talk to him with care, because the chapel would never like associating with anything that went against their doctrines, and paranormal stuff falls straight out of the realm.

After much preparation, I dialled the number.

It was a while before the call got connected, and even as it rang, I had the mental image of an old landline ringing somewhere far away in the confines of some long, lonely corridor. After about ten rings, the phone was picked up.

'Hello, good evening. I am Jay Alani from Mumbai. Could I speak with Father Francis?'

'I am Father Francis,' said a stern voice. 'What is this about?'

'Father, I wish to visit the Three Kings Chapel,' I said without mincing words.

'Why?'

'I just want to look at it for a project.'

'That's nice,' said the parson. 'Are you some kind of reporter? We welcome reporters who could throw some light on this much-neglected part of Goa.'

I was about to correct him, but then I decided to play along. 'Father, could you tell me something about the chapel?'

The priest promptly launched into a very helpful narration about the chapel's architecture and its relevance in the contemporary social culture of the village. 'You should actually come in the first week of January when we conduct the Three Kings Festival,' he said finally. 'That's when you will see everything in its full glory.'

'I will visit again at that time,' I lied. 'But, father, I have heard some things about the chapel.'

There was a moment's hesitation before he said, 'What things?'

'Actually, father, I read several articles on the Internet about the chapel being . . . haunted.'

A pensive pause followed. Perhaps the priest had to really think hard for a suitable response.

'You should not believe in those, son. You know how the Internet is. People will post anything.'

I tried my luck and pressed on. 'Father, I met with some people here who stayed back in the chapel one evening. They saw some really strange things.'

'Don't believe them!' he said, almost chiding me. 'No one can stay in the chapel in the evening. We lock it.'

I made one last-ditch attempt. 'Father, would it be okay if I come to Three Kings to study it?'

'What study? Are you really a reporter?'

'No, father. I am a paranormal investigator.'

Now, close to being very angry, the priest said, 'I cannot talk to you any further, son. The chapel does not believe in such things, and we do not feel it appropriate to communicate with those who do. May God show you the light.'

With that, the line went dead. I felt a strong urge to call him again, but resisted. I knew he wouldn't be of any more help. I'd have to find the answers on my own.

———

Throughout the flight and the subsequent journey to the Three Kings Chapel, Vikas and Sunidhi shocked me with further instances of things that had transpired with them over the past year. The damp patch was now a prime topic of discussion, with Sunidhi remarking how that patch seemed to change shape every time she saw it.

The couple were definitely going through a rough time and even revisiting their relationship itself, I could tell. But then I also knew that if I got to the bottom of this and the negative energy indeed left them at Three Kings as I supposed it would, it would very likely rekindle the spark between them. I hoped for the best.

I asked them if they felt anything of the presence then, during the flight, but they said they did not. Vikas told me that they were all right when they were outside the house.

That would make it difficult then. If the spirit, or whatever it was, wasn't travelling back with them, it would be difficult to deliver it back to Three Kings. I hoped as hard as I could that the spirit was indeed with them and hadn't made their house its new abode.

We checked into the hotel, freshened up and I talked to them about heading off to the chapel right away. There was not much time to waste. We had come on an afternoon flight, which left us with just the right amount of time to reach the chapel before sundown and wait there until the doors were shut, after which we could sneak our way in.

I know that sneaking into a place of worship is wrong, and I was just as scandalized as you might be now when I first heard of Vikas and Sunidhi's breaking into the chapel. But the stakes were higher now. After that talk with Father Francis, getting any kind of permission to spend time in the chapel was impossible. On the other hand, there was this young couple, tormented out of their wits by something that they could not explain. I had to make a choice, and I made one that made my conscience feel better.

It was dusk when we stood in front of the monument. There was a moment when Vikas tried to convince me to go forth alone, that they were not needed. I could see the fear in his eyes as he spoke. I could imagine what he was going through. He had experienced three ghostly apparitions there and they had sucked the energy out of him. Reliving that would be immensely painful for someone like him who was not attuned to the paranormal the way I was. But I had to persuade him. I told him that the entity had latched on to them, probably particularly on *him*, because he was the one who scrambled out of that chapel window last, and that was why it was important that he go inside.

His only assurance was me standing next to him, equipped with a backpack filled with assorted paranormal-investigation equipment.

I noticed his legs were trembling; I could feel the warm air he was exhaling in short bursts. Sunidhi held his hand firmly, as if encouraging him, but I knew she was shivering within. And I will not lie. As I stood in front of that all-white building situated at that altitude, jutting out starkly against everything else in the landscape, I felt a twinge of nervousness in my heart too.

I saw them hold each other's hands.

'What are we supposed to do?' asked Sunidhi.

'All we have to do is get into the chapel somehow,' I said, looking firmly at the huge iron lock on the door. That feeling of intense sorrow had gripped me again. I did not know what I was getting myself into. But I did not want to scare the couple any further and kept my thoughts to myself.

Vikas nodded tersely and started walking in the direction of the window. I followed.

Just then, I heard some movement behind me. I turned back to look, and it was a man with a stout stick in his hands. Vikas gestured with his hands to tell me that it was the same person who had met them a year ago.

'We just want to take a look inside,' I told the man.

'The chapel is closed,' said the man in a tone that left no doubt about who was in charge.

'Look, sir,' Vikas attempted, 'all we want to do is see the altar once.'

'You don't understand,' said the man, glaring. 'The chapel is closed. Please leave.'

Vikas started to say something, but I signalled to him to stay quiet.

'Okay, we will leave,' I told the man. 'Sorry to bother you.'

Saying that, I turned. We went back to the main road where we had parked our bikes and waited.

'What's our plan of action?' Sunidhi asked.

I threw down the cigarette I had been smoking. 'Where's that window you had entered from?'

It was getting darker now. We scoped the place a bit to make sure there was no one around. I knew that this was wrong, but there was no other way. Anyway, I didn't expect it to be a long visit.

We found the window. It was jammed shut, but still unlocked. As I pushed it inwards, it made a faint creaking noise as it yielded. Breathing heavily, I climbed into the chapel.

———

The chapel was every bit as scary as I expected from all that I had read about it. I wanted to scold Vikas and Sunidhi right then and there for being so idiotic as to spend a night there. Truth be told, we can keep most troubles away by not being reckless. But then youth is reckless and so is love, and both together make a dangerous combination. So here I was, trying to sort out their problem.

I kept my backpack on the floor and unzipped it. I took out my infrared thermometer, K2 meter and flashlight and started walking around. The couple followed me, two steps behind, fascinated.

I handed over the thermometer to Vikas. 'Will you be able to handle this?'

'I . . . I don't know how . . .' He looked like a little boy holding a new toy; the fear I had seen on his face a moment ago had vanished.

'This is just a thermometer,' I told him. 'It's a probe thermometer. It records temperature. If you press this button here, the backlight will tell you the reading. All you have to do is see if there are any cold spots.'

'Cold spots?' Sunidhi asked.

'If there are spirits, they can alter the temperature. A cold spot indicates their presence.'

Both of them shuddered visibly. The fear was back.

'Where did you see the shadows?' I whispered.

They pointed out the last pew. I walked to it slowly, the light from my torch falling on the various paintings on the wall, uncannily distorting the colours, giving them a surreal look. Highly alert now and trying not to bump into anything, I kept my eyes peeled to observe not just my equipment but also any changes around the couple. Whatever was to happen would happen around them.

'Do . . . do you see anything?' Vikas asked me.

'Not yet. But hold steady.'

We reached the back of the chapel hall. My entire attention was on the K2 meter and I kept staring at it, not wanting to miss the slightest flicker of light. At one point, I froze when three lights began blinking in a pattern. One light, three lights, one light, three lights.

'Wh-what's happening?' Vikas whispered.

'Something's here.'

As the lights kept up, I lowered myself on to the pew, gesturing Vikas to sit at the other end. Sunidhi sat between us, and we stayed as still as we could for several minutes. The play of lights continued. They must have been itching to ask me tons of questions, but I was glad they didn't. We had to be as non-confrontational as possible.

'Is anyone here?' I asked in a gentle voice. 'You are making your presence felt. Do you wish to tell us anything?'

My eyes were fixed on the lights. There was no difference in the way they moved. One light, three lights, one light, three lights, it went on. It was really a highly curious pattern I haven't seen in any other place.

'I have come here with Vikas and Sunidhi,' I continued. 'They trespassed on your property a year ago, and maybe unknowingly took back something from here. I request you to take it back from them now and leave them in peace.'

Again, nothing unusual happened. At this point, I knew that there were spirits and that they were listening to me. But I did not know if they understood.

Now, apart from the lights, I did feel a presence even going by mere instinct. There was no question that there was something in there. Was it the souls of the kings or something else, I did not know. My theory was that there would be a reunion of sorts here; that the spirit haunting the couple's house would unlatch himself in the chapel and reunite with his brothers. I counted on that to happen, but you cannot order spirits to do your bidding. Also, I did not know for sure whether it would happen at all.

'You two sit here,' I told them and stood up.

Something had caught my attention—the altar.

I had sensed a faint movement there. A motion capture device could have recorded something, but I was not carrying one.

The altar was decorated as if in preparation for a Mass to be conducted the next morning. I imagined what it must have been like in the years gone by when people might actually have been sitting here, listening to a priest giving a sermon from that altar, and then I was blinded. A bright flash of light beamed right into my eyes. As I shut my eyes to shield them, I had a psychic vision for the first time in my life. A vision of a priest dressed in white with a red sash, standing tall at that altar and preaching to an audience attired in centuries-old clothes. But when I opened my eyes, the altar was again barren and dark. I looked behind at Vikas and Sunidhi. They were sitting still, unaffected. I knew then that only I had had the vision.

I moved up and targeted my K2 meter at the altar. I was just about 10 feet from it now. My flashlight was off.

Just then, the lights moved.

This time it was terrifying. All five lights came on at once, and stayed on. This was a high activity field.

I stepped back slowly and signalled to Vikas to stand. 'Get that thermometer.'

Vikas almost crawled up to me. His hand shook as he held the thermometer. I told him to bravely go near the altar. He took about four steps and almost fainted.

The thermometer reading had dipped. Significantly.

'What does this mean?' he asked breathlessly.

'Stay right where you are, Vikas.'

'What . . . It's cold here . . .'

Sunidhi came up to me. 'What's happening?' she asked, her voice hoarse.

'Don't panic, Sunidhi,' I told her, holding her hand.

'What?' she almost screamed.

'Shh!' I clamped her mouth with one hand.

Vikas, meanwhile, was numb with shock. He stood as if paralysed. I had never before seen something like this. From where we watched, it appeared as if he was just standing there, rooted to the spot like an insensate statue.

'What can he see? Does he see something?' Sunidhi whispered to me. Her eyes had an indescribably frightful look.

I knew *exactly* what was happening to him. But I could not say it out loud, otherwise I risked them reacting in unpredictable ways. Fear makes you do strange things.

What was happening with Vikas was that he had walked right into the ethereal form of the spirit.

My K2 meter was going crazy. Right above Vikas's head, Sunidhi and I could see black wisps beginning to take shape.

I had to think fast. I could only imagine his state. He was an inch away from collapsing.

And then there was a loud banging on the chapel door.

Who's inside?' came an angry voice.

I turned sharply to the door to look. When I looked back at Vikas, the wisps were gone.

'Stay calm,' I told the couple. 'Looks like it's that chapel guard.'

Sunidhi ran up to Vikas and held him. As I walked to the door, I saw his dazed form. His face had gone very pale now.

The chapel door was still locked. Apparently, the person outside did not have the key.

'Who is inside?' the angry voice repeated. 'Speak up. We know someone is in there.'

We. There was more than one person outside.

I opened my mouth to answer, then decided against it. In a hurry, I walked up to Sunidhi and said, 'They don't know for sure we are here. Let's leave this place immediately.'

'But . . . Vikas?'

Vikas was white as a sheet, but he was still standing.

'He'll be fine,' I said. 'But let's get away. Facing an angry group of people is never a good idea.'

We heard the clanging of the lock now. Someone had apparently got the key.

'I hate to be sneaky like this,' I said, 'but hurry now. Go out.'

Sunidhi ran up to the window, practically dragging a severely disoriented Vikas behind her. Helping him out of the window, she clambered out of it too. I saw Vikas getting back on his feet. Seeing that they were out, I ran behind them too, and with one leg out of the window, I turned to look into the chapel one last time. Something had happened there, for sure. I looked at where the aura had engulfed Vikas, and I only hoped the thing we had come for had been accomplished.

I shut the window just as I heard the door being forced open amid furious shouts.

———

Vikas called me a month later. I had moved on to other things and was giving a talk in another city when the call came. It took me a moment to recognize his voice; it had changed that much. It had changed for the better.

'We don't know how to thank you, Jay sir,' he said. 'Whatever we tried to do there, it helped. Our happy days are back, and I cannot thank you enough.'

'That's good to hear,' I said. 'I didn't ask you at that time, but can you tell me what you saw that night?'

There was some hesitation before he replied.

'I . . . I cannot really describe it. It was . . . like some black smoke all around me and I felt something going out from my body. I don't know what, but I was very, very sad for a moment. Like I wanted to kill myself. And then it was gone, leaving me with an empty feeling.'

I was smiling as I disconnected the call. This case had weighed on my conscience, for I had done things I sure am not proud of, like sneaking into a locked sacred place, but it had turned out to be for a just cause after all.

All is well that ends well, as they say.

9

The Headless Boy of Mussoorie

ONE OF THE most extraordinary legends I have ever come across was during my 2018 tour of Mussoorie. This was the story of a headless boy who roams the dense deodar forests at night. Locals claim that the cries of the boy can still be heard, and no one ventures there after dark. When I heard of this, I could not resist spending a night in the jungle in the hope of finding out more. Was the apparition just a figment of some creative local imagination or indeed a restive spirit who needed deliverance?

To get answers, I made the trip on a bitterly cold December night. Battling against many natural odds, I managed to reach a point where things became clearer. The following is an account of my explorations into this terrifying forest.

In December 2018, I was in Mussoorie, taking my time and exploring the rich trove of paranormally active locations in the valley. During my travels, I came to know of a tragically shocking legend. It is said that the forests surrounding

Mussoorie are haunted by the ghost of a headless boy who roams about in the night. The tale is so common in these parts that people do not take this route after nightfall any longer. Some claim that the boy creeps up behind unwary travellers and drags them into the middle of the forest, where he decapitates them. Some others believe he has colossal strength; they even say that his form can grow up to 20 feet high in front of any unfortunate person who might happen to cross paths with him.

With all these stories afloat, I surely could not give this place a miss. My sojourn in Mussoorie was coming to an end, but I decided to stretch it by a couple of days to get to the bottom of the mystery, hoping to perhaps even get a glimpse of this peculiar ghost that had terrorized the regions skirting the forest.

I had only sketchy information to start with. People did not want to talk about it, but I could elicit some idea of the location from a tourist guide at the hotel I was staying in. He told me, 'Oh, you wish to see the headless boy's ghost. Well, to each their own! Take the road that goes from Mussoorie to Dhanaulti. About one hour ahead, you will see a side road that goes to the right. Take that route and go further by about a kilometre. You will be in a dense forest with tall deodar trees. This is the place where he is known to lurk.' When I thanked him, he said, 'Memorize the *Hanuman Chalisa* before you leave, if you don't know it yet.'

Realizing that I would have to find everything on my own, I rented a motorbike and set out a bit early in the evening. But the road was long and winding, and I could not see any side road of the kind the guide had suggested. I stopped at a roadside stall selling tea and cigarettes, run by a middle-aged man. His head and ears were covered with a thick red shawl. I asked him for tea and then opened conversation.

'*Bhaiya*, do you know any forest here?'

'Which forest?' he asked.

He seemed interested in talking, so I decided to be upfront.

'I have heard there is a ghost in these parts.'

At that, his face suddenly turned white. He pulled the shawl closer around his ears as if affected by a sudden chill.

'You know about it?' I asked.

'Why do you want him?'

The way he said *him* sounded odd. As if the ghost and he were long-lost buddies. 'I am a researcher,' I said. 'I like to find out about things.'

He shook his head. 'It is not far from here. Around fifteen minutes. Keep your eyes on the right. It's a very narrow road. You might miss it.'

'Thank you! Do you know anything about him?'

He shuddered. 'It is too late in the night to talk about *him*.'

I looked at my watch. It was 9 p.m. The tea shop would probably remain open for another hour. And there was that intimidating reverence in his tone again.

'I don't get scared,' I said.

He laughed. 'I was not talking about you.'

I stayed quiet, trying to smile back at him.

He decided to oblige. He took a cigarette from a pack that was on sale and offered me another, before he continued.

'His name was Dipak. He was the son of a wood gatherer who lived here around twenty years ago. His father would collect wood from the forest and sell it to the factories. One night, when his father was late returning home, Dipak went out to look for him. But it was dark. The boy got lost. He saw four other woodcutters and asked them to guide him to the main road. But the men were drunk and full of lust. Seeing that this boy was such easy prey, they took him deeper into the jungle. And there they—'

The man's voice faltered. I shuddered at the thought of what was coming, and then he spelt it out.

'The men took turns raping the fourteen-year-old. When they were done with their evil deed, they strangled the boy and tried to kill him. But the boy did not die. Then one of the four did something horrible. The bastard took his axe and chopped off the boy's head.'

'Oh goodness!' I said aloud. This was beyond anything I had imagined.

'Sahib, Mussoorie is a calm and peaceful place. Crimes almost never happen here. When news of this one spread, people could not sleep for months due to the sheer brutality of it. People still never talk about it. To know that they could not protect a child of their own is a matter of great dishonour to all of us here.'

'What happened to the men?'

'Nature has its strange ways. Seven days later, one of the men, the one who chopped off the boy's head, was found dead in the forest, and mysteriously enough, in the exact same place where the boy was killed. The other three men were never found.' His voice dipped as he said, 'The death of that one man in such mysterious circumstances was enough proof that the child was back in the form of a ghost. And so the stories began.'

I bid the man goodbye and got my motorcycle. There was nothing sane I could think of right then, for my mind was in a whirl. Ghost or not, I could hear the child's screams, so affected was I by that sordid tale. How can anyone be so brutal to a child, and just to satisfy their momentary urges? When did we, as a species, fall so low?

Plunged deep in thought, I hit a small bump on the road. It was as if that little incident was preordained, for I turned, on reflex, to my right and saw a clear detour leading on from the main road. Heeding the call of the unexplained, I rode away into the heart of the unknown.

———

I had gone about 500 metres into the jungle. I couldn't bring my motorcycle much farther into the side road, for it had soon devolved into a mud path riddled with pebbles and twigs. I strapped on my equipment bag, which contained my regular tools—K2 meter, infrared thermometer, sound sensors, cameras—and continued on foot, relying purely on my instincts. All around me were tall deodar trees. Their musty fragrance was invigorating and gave me a heady feeling. And it was cold—terribly, terribly cold. I already had one sweater on, but I feared that I was underprepared and that this might not be enough against the bitter and unrelenting forest chill.

It was absolutely dark now. It was a couple of days before the full moon, but the canopy of leaves from the tall trees shielded the moonlight. To add to that, there was a rising mist. As I walked further, the mist grew denser. I did not realize when it got so hazy that I could not see my own hands.

There was something else I had noticed and alerted myself to be cautious of—the stray dogs of the jungle. I saw them in ones and in twos and in groups, and they were scattered all over the place. As I walked by, the twigs underfoot making a crunching sound, they turned sharply to look at me and stared. I tried to soften my steps, reminding myself that these weren't city dogs. They were savage and I was encroaching on to their territory. But the animals looked benign, at least for now. Their eyes lingered on me for a moment and then they looked away. At every instant, I was worried that one of them might start barking. If one did, then I knew the others would follow, and I would not know how to save myself from an army of feral canines.

The foliage was thick and any rare clearing that came up was a blessing. Broad tree trunks were almost everywhere, and they grew so high that I could not see their tops. It did not take long for me to lose all sense of direction. In most places, I could not even see the night stars. However, being in the hills, the terrain was uneven. At one point, I climbed what appeared to be a rocky incline and could see the nearby mountainscape. I spotted something in the distance, a faint shimmering. Intrigued, I looked more closely and realized that it was the city of Mussoorie I had left behind. The glittering was the night lights of the city.

This buoyed my spirits, as it gave me some sense of direction, but it also caused concern. It told me that I was miles away from the city now, or any significant human civilization, so to speak.

Trying not to lose sight of the lights on the mountain, and holding that as my directional guide, I walked on ahead. Somewhere in the distance, there was a sharp barking. I froze for a moment, worrying that the creature might have barked at me. But it turned out to be a distant sound, far away enough for it to echo in the valley. This was followed by another bark. And then another. One of them seemed to come from just a few metres away. Standing there in the jungle alone at that unearthly hour, surrounded by hundreds of wild dogs that I could not see, and the prospect of coming up against a headless boy at any instant, was probably the most frightening experience I have had during my investigations.

What was more nerve-wracking was that I did not know where I had to go. This was a much bigger area than I had anticipated, and it was as sylvan as nature had made it. In most jungles in India, we find human traces everywhere—plastic wrappers, names etched into tree barks, pieces of cloth or papers strewn about. But here there was nothing that even remotely reminded me of another human besides me. I had walked so deep inside now that dried leaves and twigs lay scattered on the ground everywhere. Here and there I could get a whiff of animal faeces. Insects glowed all around me, some of them hitting against my face. There might have been snakes slithering close to me, but I took every step carefully and I was in tall boots, a precaution I always take when stepping into thick vegetation.

I don't know if you have ever had that feeling—the feeling of being in a place untouched by other humans. It is a feeling that completely overwhelms you, that takes you to the pinnacle of exhilaration, and if you come out of it in one piece, it will give you a high every time you think of it. I had that very feeling in the Mussoorie jungle.

And to add to it was the feeling that I was undertaking this highly risky journey with no necessary purpose, except to satiate my innate curiosity for the unknown and my incessant urge for answers.

It took me a while to shake off these thoughts and concentrate on the task at hand. The animal sounds had been growing. There was a continual shrill cry of some animal or perhaps a nightbird that pierced through the mist and echoed several times all around. It was so sharp that it rattled my brain every time I heard it. There was also an alarming regularity in the way it was issued; a gap of about ten seconds prevailed between two calls. It was unlike anything I had ever heard, and I hoped I could catch a glimpse of whatever that creature was. At least that could be something to take away from this trip.

Then, when I had been walking for about two hours, strictly keeping the distant city lights to my right, I heard something that was different from all the other jungle sounds. A footfall. The delicate sound of a foot treading on the forest ground behind me.

I turned—

I cannot fully describe the horror of the sound of a single footstep right behind you when you are alone in a desolate forest at night.

The sound was distinct—heavy and somewhat squishy, like what a rubber chappal would make on wet sand. For a moment, I stood rooted to the spot, trying to see if whatever it was made another move. After a minute, I turned on my cell- phone flashlight. So far, I had been moving only in the ambient light, going by instinct, for it did not feel right somehow to adulterate this natural habitat with electronic devices.

But even with the flashlight, it was difficult to see much; the mist was so strong. Thick and opaque, all I could see was the glint of many forest insects. They were out in millions here, undeterred by any human presence, flitting away in abandon. I took a few paces ahead and then stood still. There was a shape under a large tree.

Being very cautious now, I asked in a soft voice, '*Kaun hai vahaan* [Who is there]?'

There was no answer. The shape looked like a mound, and it was completely static. Was this the headless ghost? Suddenly, as I moved ahead, very guardedly, I felt it grow colder. It was already biting cold, but I was coming to a spot where it was much more severe. I could feel the iciness seep in through my sweater and my flesh, cutting right into my bone. I could feel it penetrate my brain through my skull. It made me shiver like I never had before.

I stepped back. All of a sudden, it was warmer.

Even in that death-defying state, that millisecond variation stunned me. I took one step ahead gingerly and the murderous cold was back, causing my knees to knock against each other. I stepped back again, and it was warmer once more.

It was as if the cold was a shield preventing me from going ahead and reaching that mound, whatever it was.

I took out my infrared thermometer. My hands weren't steady now, and the red laser light danced all over the place. Mustering all my strength, I stepped into the frigid zone and then stepped back. The result left me unable to breathe. There was a variation of 4 degrees between the two spots.

This was undoubtedly the spot.

Steeling every nerve and fibre in my body, I decided to go back to the cold spot. I had to reach the mound. This was dangerous, but this was also the kind of thing we paranormal investigators live for. I could face any kind of haunting, but I could never live down being haunted by the thought that I had come so close and backed away.

Telling myself there was nothing to lose, I stepped in.

The cold wave engulfed me like a monster grabbing me with its tentacles.

I could not even open my eyes fully, for the mist hit me like a hundred cold-tipped needles. Somehow, I managed to peer ahead, but I relied more on my arms which I now swung ahead of me like a blinded person might. Careful so as not to sway from my path, I took a few more steps in a straight line and then I felt something.

My eyes flew open and I saw what the mound really was. I gasped.

It was a strange kind of rock, perfectly propped up against the tree, which I now realized was a banyan tree. When I shone my flashlight on it, I fell back in astonishment. There was orange and red powder smeared on the rock. Furthermore, there was a framed photograph at the foot of the rock. The photograph was of a smiling boy. A garland of long-wilted flowers was around it.

This was a shrine built for the poor boy.

Who could have built it here? Maybe his family? The boy looked so real, so lifelike in that photograph, as if he were still smiling at me. Somehow, it exacerbated the violence of the act he had suffered in his short life. It threw me into such despair that for a moment, I simply forgot the cold.

Another terrifying thought seized me at that moment—this was probably the exact spot where the boy had been brutalized and killed. I had reached the place where he had gone into his spirit form.

Standing there, I could feel him looking at me. Perhaps assessing who I was.

———

Not able to bear it any more, I stepped back from the cold spot and flopped right there on the ground. There was no energy left in me. I was breathing heavily and didn't know how much more I could take it. Yet another shock awaited me. I saw the time. It was 2.45 a.m. I checked both my phone and my watch to be sure. This made me sit up because I was sure it was 11.30 when I stepped into the cold zone. Where did I lose the three hours?

There was no way I had spent three hours scanning that cold spot. At best, it could have only been fifteen minutes.

A chill seeped in at the nape of my neck. I had heard that spirits could manipulate time, but this was the first time that it had happened to me. I was seeing it, right there, right then, and there was no explanation whatsoever for it.

Reaching into my backpack, I finally took out the most decisive device I had with me at the moment—my K2 meter. Until now, I had had no need of it, but for what I was going to do, I needed something visual; just my instincts wouldn't do any more.

Under normal circumstances, the K2 meter shows one of its five lights lit up. Here, in this jungle, you could not have expected an electromagnetic field to fire up any more lights, but I was ready for anything now.

I plunged the K2 meter into the cold spot as if I were jabbing a dagger into the mist.

Almost immediately, all five lights lit up.

Taking the instrument back, and drawing in a deep breath, I decided to start the communication. Politely, I asked in Hindi, 'Is anyone here?'

The lights lit up.

I was amazed. This was a matter of great wonder. I was both frightened and fascinated. Even in that situation, I had the thought of saving this moment for posterity somehow.

'Are you Dipak?' My voice was clear and concise, despite the slight trembling due to the cold. Still, I ensured that I did not give out any hint that I was afraid. Spirits suck on negative energies.

The lights lit up again.

It was Dipak! The headless boy was around somewhere. I was talking to him! I couldn't see him yet, but there was this dense fog all around.

'Dipak?' I said, and waited for a second. Angry spirits mellow down when addressed by name. 'I know what happened to you. I am terribly hurt and saddened by it. I want you to know that you are a brave boy who went into the jungle looking for your father. I am sure your father misses you a lot. Do you hear me, Dipak?'

Only the second light lit up this time. It was as if my words were hitting home.

'Dipak, I am a good guy too. I wish to be your friend. I do not want to harm you. Will you show yourself to me?'

I knew I was asking too much. I was challenging him. Stories of other people being killed by this headless boy came back to me, but I had done nothing to incite his ire. It was a daring step that I needed to take.

For a while, there was nothing on the K2 meter.

'Please, can you show me any sign that you are here?'

Something happened on the K2 meter.

'Will you show yourself to me?'

There was no response.

I thought of asking about the other three rapists who were still missing, but I didn't. It is never a good idea to remind a friendly spirit about the way they died. It can cause their energies to turn hostile. I silently resigned myself to the thought that the three men might still be alive somewhere, because otherwise there was no reason for Dipak's spirit to remain here. Maybe he could not leave this spot. That one person who was killed may have strayed here, and then maybe the others kept away out of sheer fright.

However, I wanted Dipak to show himself in a more tangible manner. Also, I was challenging myself to see how far I could go. How much I had evolved as an investigator, so to speak. After a few minutes of silence, I made another attempt.

'Dipak, are you still here?'

The lights did not come up immediately this time, but they slightly jumped about ten seconds later.

'I am still waiting here,' I said. 'I really want to see more of you.'

There was no response on the meter. By this time, my bones had grown warmer. My brain had thawed. I thought of entering the cold zone again, and probably going farther this time, beyond the mound, for that is where I assumed the boy was. Maybe this could stimulate him to manifest. But it would be a rather bold step. It would be like stepping right into his lair, and he might not like the intrusion. Still, it was a once-in-a-lifetime chance that I did not want to miss.

I stood up and thrust the K2 meter into my pocket. Shrugging off the numbness, I moved into the spot again. The cold gripped me instantly, but this time I was better prepared for it, and having come out of it once, I was more confident too. I tried to speak, but my words came out in a halting quiver.

'Dipak . . . I am coming closer to you now. Do not be afraid. I just want to . . . see you.'

I moved, one step at a time, aware of some faint music playing somewhere. It was like a flute, and it was a haunting melody. Who would be playing a flute of all things in the middle of the forest at night? I brushed away the thought. Maybe the cold was making me hallucinate. I took another step forward.

I reached the mound and stopped. The next step was going to be a decisive one. It was complete darkness here, the ground was squelchy and I could not see any of it because of the darkness and the fog. It was highly risky not knowing what I was stepping on, but I was determined.

Suddenly, I sensed a movement behind me.

I heard footsteps moving away. Almost running. Stranded in the fog, I could see a darker shape receding into the distance. I came out of the cold quickly and tried to look, but apart from a gap in the middle of the trees, I could see nothing.

Something came at me then, something round and hard, and hit me squarely in the chest. It was such a heavy blow that I bent over, sputtering, and as I did that, I saw an object rolling away among the trees. It looked like a football; that was all I could see of it before it vanished into the trees.

A terrifying thought gripped me. Who had thrown that at me? And was it really a football? Was it, really? I hoped and even prayed it was just a football or some fruit that had fallen from a tree and nothing more than that. But the feeling would not leave me. Just as that thing rolled out of sight, I thought I saw something on it—*why did those things look so similar to human eyes?*

I was still reeling under the shock when I heard something—the barking of dogs. It was coming from the distance and I could tell it was a number of them, for these weren't single sharp barks but a rising wave of them. And as the wave grew louder, I realized they were coming closer.

Very, very close.

Till it was such a riot that I had to cover my ears.

From between the distant trees emerged the manically charging bodies of several dogs of many shapes and sizes, and they were all headed in my direction.

It took me a split second to realize that the dogs were running right at me!

There wasn't a moment to lose. Despite the fact that my legs were half-frozen, I turned and started to run in the opposite direction. I tripped and fell, but I picked myself up and kept running. The longer I did this, the warmer I got, and the more I was able to run. I picked up speed, and fled like a horse in the woods, not minding the brushes and cuts against the shrubbery. I let myself go like never before.

The barking of a hundred dogs was upon me. I could feel it swelling with every passing step, as more and more of those untamed creatures might have joined the bandwagon.

I did not know which direction I was running in and had absolutely no clue where I had parked my bike. All I had in that moment was an insanely heightened degree of survival instinct.

Somewhere along the way, I saw a hole in a rock. It was higher than the ground, but I could reach it and wedge myself in there. If I managed to get there, I would live to tell the tale.

Using all my athletic abilities, I took that sharp detour and parkoured my way to the top where the hole was. Hoping that it wasn't a bear's lair or a python's hideout, I let myself go in. Half my body went inside, while the other half stayed out, but I was well out of reach of the dogs.

And when the dogs came at me, it was a sight to behold. They were easily a hundred, all thick and furry, fed on the meat the jungles provided so plentifully. Their fangs were bared, their eyes were full of bloodlust and their strong limbs were bursting with energy. Some of them tried to climb up to where I was, but they slid down after the first few steps. Slowly, when I realized I was safe, if only trapped, I allowed myself to breathe. Soon, the morning would dawn and, hopefully, these animals would give up and leave.

———

I made my way out of the forest in the morning. My bike was parked kilometres away, but at least I was on the main road circling the jungle. I kept to it. I trekked all the way till I found my bike, and as I began to ride away from there, the first wave of the thrill really hit me.

This was as close to being mauled to death as I had ever come. Today, when I retrospect on that entire episode, it still makes my hair stand on end, but it also tells me that I did something not many men would. And, most importantly, I might have come the closest to a spirit in all my paranormal career.

I still think about Dipak. His face in that photograph is firmly etched in my memory. That innocence snatched away in such a grotesque and evil manner—and for what? Just to satisfy a few minutes of lust? Only a human being can be that evil to another human being. Yes, even more evil than those raging packs of dogs that wanted to tear me from limb to limb. For the dogs were doing it out of the sheer need for survival. What justification did the rapists have to defend themselves anyway?

I will say this on record that I am happy that Dipak could get one of his rapists. I wish sometimes that he gets to the other three too, if he hasn't already.

But one question lingers in my mind. Why did he decide to communicate with me? I suppose spirits also get lonely sometimes, and he just wanted to share his burden momentarily. He probably found me a safe person to talk to. He didn't show me his rumoured legendary form, but that's perhaps just that—a legend built on hearsay. He got scared and attacked me, and maybe he was the one who set the dogs on me as I had overstayed my welcome, but that is also understandable. Maybe there is no physical form of him around any more. None of those stories of him being 20 feet tall are real. Maybe that little shrine is all he has.

And he was right to protect it. Even from me.

10

Temple of Exorcism

THIS EXPERIENCE WHICH I share with you here is something I encountered at a very famous temple held in great esteem by people of the faith. For that reason, I was in two minds about whether I wanted to talk about it. After a lot of thought, I decided to share the story with you, but without actually naming the temple. All names of places and people in this story are fictional.

Maybe one day I shall be able to share this story with complete honesty. Until then, this is what I can offer you. I hope you will bear with me.

Among the many sobriquets accorded to our great nation, 'Land of Temples' occupies a chief position. It is said that one cannot walk for more than ten minutes anywhere in India without coming across a religious structure of some kind. But where religious folks are found in such great numbers, there is also an industry that takes undue advantage of people's beliefs. Some places of worship have turned into hubs for nefarious practices in the guise of religion. In this story, I am going to tell you about one such shrine where hair-raising incidents take place even today, and which are patronized in vast measure by people's credulity.

This temple, situated in the heart of a prominent upcoming city of India, is famous for two things. One is its magnificent architecture, which draws people, both local and foreign, in droves. In fact, in the holiday months of April–May, it is difficult to set foot in the precincts. The other reason why it is famous is rather sinister. It is known to be a venue for terrifying exorcisms, all of which are performed ritualistically in the presence of thousands of devotees.

I first visited the place when I was barely sixteen. I had gone with my parents to the city and we spent a couple of hours at the temple as part of our itinerary. Until then, I knew nothing of the practices that were conducted in those halls, but what I witnessed that day left an indelible mark on my mind.

The scene was right out of a Bollywood movie.

The temple had a huge palatial hall where devotees would assemble during the rites. I remember standing there amidst a huge crowd of people chattering away and a continuous, dissonant chanting of mantras coming from somewhere near the sanctum sanctorum. It was around six in the evening, the *sandhya* hour. The idol of the deity stood in the altar striking a fearsome pose and was decorated with several garlands ensconced in the swirling smoke of incense sticks burning away on either side. The ringing of the bells was deafening. It seemed to be some kind of festive occasion that we did not know of. That's hardly surprising as, in India, every day is a festival in some part or the other.

Suddenly, a hush fell over the crowd. All movement and chanting came to a halt and the ringing of bells ceased. People made way and a path was created that went directly from the gates of the temple to the main altar. A tall and imposing man walked in. He was bald and dressed in a single, folded white cloth that hung from his shoulders and came up to his knees. His forehead bore several marks of devotion and the immense rings adorning both his ears caught my attention. He strode into the hall in a perfect, unhindered gait and took his position by the altar. Someone in the crowd said that the Mahanta (the chief priest) had arrived. The Mahanta is a sort of chief priest of a temple. All major ceremonies are conducted either by him or under his direct guidance.

As people watched with bated breath, there was the sound of crying from somewhere in the distance. The crying grew louder and, with every rising wail, a new wave of terror rippled through my veins. Something was approaching. No one was looking at the Mahanta now. Their sights were fixed on the gates, from which several people, both men and women, came forth. The men were dressed in similar temple robes, and they were dragging the women by their hair into the temple.

I was shocked. I had never seen such a public display of manhandling before.

The women were the ones crying, but no one was paying any heed to them. The men dragged them all the way across the temple, from the gates to the altar, where they left the women writhing on the floor and then assembled behind the Mahanta.

The next thing I remember is a man, as heavily built as an executioner but dressed in the same white temple robes, readying a stout stick as if for some kind of battle. Terrified, I turned away.

I was later told that the women were possessed. What I had witnessed was an exorcism rite.

———

About ten years later, in 2016, I received a call that would rekindle the horrific memories of what I had witnessed at that temple. A lot had happened over these years. I had taken up an active paranormal-investigation career, having been trained by experts from across the world. I had featured in television shows and given talks on the subject. My records of investigations conducted in some of the most popular paranormally active locations of India were in the public domain, such as on podcasts and YouTube and Instagram. Owing to my efforts in spreading awareness about this unknown world, I had started receiving calls from people across the country to come and inspect places that were known for some or the other unexplained activity.

Early one morning, I received a call. The person on the line introduced himself as Vishnu. Like many others, he began by telling me that there was a place he knew which he thought I'd like to visit. By now, I had become selective when dealing with such calls, but then he mentioned something that made me sit up. He said that the place he had in mind was this temple.

I did not tell him that I knew about the temple. I waited to hear what he had to say.

'This is a very strange temple, Jay bhai,' he said. 'Here, exorcisms happen openly. I have seen one, and they are terrifying. You should come and take a look. I will guide you.'

I hesitated a while, as if thinking of a suitable reply. Truth be told, that one experience I had at the temple had scarred me so badly that I did not really want to go there again. But then there was another part of me that urged me to go. I had faced all my demons in life, and I should not leave this one chapter unfinished, I thought, especially since I had now become an investigator of the bizarre. I decided that this would be as good an opportunity as any to go back to the site.

I told him, 'All right, I will come. But will they allow me to record anything in the temple?'

'I don't know about that, bhai. But I could give you the number of a man named Mahendra Swami. He is the son of the trustee of the temple. He is also one of the swamis of the temple. I think, with your reputation, it's better if you speak with him.'

That sounded fair. I took the number from Vishnu and told him that I would get back to him shortly.

I immediately called Mahendra Swami. As the phone rang, I decided to assume a false identity. Somehow, I had an odd feeling about this.

'Hello, am I speaking to Mahendra Swami?' I asked in chaste Hindi, as politely as I could.

'Yes,' said a gruff voice. I had imagined the man to be young, but the voice belonged to a much-older man.

'Swamiji, I am Anil Dubey from Delhi. I wish to visit the temple,' I said, changing my name to protect my identity.

'The temple welcomes all,' he said.

'I have heard a lot about the unique rituals that are conducted. If you give me your gracious permission, I would like to record—'

'Absolutely not!' he thundered.

'Sir . . .'

'We do not allow any kind of recording in the temple premises. No photography. You cannot even carry your mobile phone. It is absolutely against our rules and an insult to the thousands of devotees who wish to pray in private in the sanctity of our temple.'

He slammed down the phone, not allowing me to talk any further.

I called Vishnu. 'They do not allow any recording,' I told him.

Vishnu pondered in silence. 'I thought so, Jay bhai,' he said simply, and that exasperated me a bit. If he knew they would deny permission, why did he put me through the rigmarole of calling them up and being reprimanded? 'But, bhai, could you please still come?' he went on. 'Even just seeing the proceedings is a huge experience. I will guide you through every detail. I have seen these exorcisms before. I want to know a few things which I think only you can answer.'

I considered his request again.

'All right. When do you want me to come?'

'This Saturday?'

'Done.'

And with that, I geared up to revisit a painful memory and possibly also uncover the truth behind it.

———

I reached the temple at the appointed time of eight in the morning and found a reedy young man in black-rimmed spectacles waiting for me. Vishnu turned out to be much younger than I thought. He was about twenty-two and had a sophisticated air about him that did not truly belong to this place. And yet he told me that he was a local and had never ventured out of that town.

Our tour began. Vishnu told me that the ongoing period of Navratra was celebrated in a big way in the temple. On all these nine holy nights, various exorcisms are performed. People come from far-off places to get their supernatural issues addressed.

'Why did you insist on today?' I asked him.

'I wanted you to see. There's an exorcism today,' he said, his voice trailing off.

I sensed he was withholding some information from me. I prodded again. 'But you just said there are exorcisms to be performed on all these nine nights. Then why insist on today?'

Then he lowered his head and said sheepishly, 'It's because the person who is getting exorcised tonight is my aunt.'

'What!'

He nodded.

'But then you believe in this stuff?'

'I am the youngest in the family,' he said, a tone of helplessness evident in his voice. 'My family is quite orthodox. No one listens to the youngest, especially in matters of religious beliefs.'

I could understand that. Religion has no equal in India, and that's where half our problems arise.

'Then have you really called me to only see what's going on here? Is there no other reason?'

'Bhai, that's the only reason. There is no way out for my aunt. She has already been admitted here. But I feel it's important for you to see what really goes on at this place.'

I did not tell him that I had been here before. It still wouldn't be a wasted trip. What I had seen ten years ago was mostly through the gaps between my fingers, for I had no courage to watch it with my eyes wide open. Questions had arisen in my mind then, and I had no answers for them. Now was the time for me to find answers. I should have actually thanked the lad for the opportunity.

'I won't be able to record anything,' I told him, 'but all right. Let us begin. Can you take me to your aunt?'

'I will, but there's one thing, Jay bhai. It is not a good idea to tell people the real reason you are here. I will introduce you as my friend and that you have come here for no other reason except your devotion to the deity.'

I nodded.

Vishnu then led me to a big, open ground behind the temple where there were many white tents erected around the entire space. There were hundreds of people milling about. It was as busy as a bazaar offering discounts.

He led me to one of the tents. He clearly did not have any difficulty in finding the right tent among all of them.

There was a bed in the middle of the tent. A woman, presumably Vishnu's aunt, was lying on it, and she was surrounded by many of his family members. The woman looked really sick. Her face had an expression of doom written all over it. I gathered that she could not move much, not even her fingers. Everyone was just sitting around her; no one spoke a word. Upon Vishnu's signal, I went forward.

Vishnu introduced me to the family. 'He's my friend. He has come to see the ritual.'

I noticed that he said 'ritual' and not 'exorcism'.

'Good to see you here, *beta*,' an old man said. 'Not many young people believe in our old traditions any more.'

I merely nodded in response and went up to the aunt. Working a smile on my face, I asked her, 'What's the problem, madam? Why are you here?'

She tried to say something. I saw her eyes grow large and then come back to normal size. But no words came forth. Instead, she made a guttural sound of pain. When no one responded, as if resigned to her fate, she continued to lie on her back and let out intermittent groans. It was a sound that would strike terror in the hearts of even the most hardened of men, but here no one was listening.

I came out of the tent and turned to Vishnu. 'How can you let this happen? You can see the condition of that woman. She is sick. You need to put a stop to this.'

'Jai bhai, trust me, there is nothing that can be done. These people, my family included, are hardened zealots. If you go against them, there's no telling what they might do to you. My aunt has accepted her fate. All we can do is witness it and see how horrific things can get.'

It was both sad and anger-inducing—not to mention frightening. Ghosts don't frighten me, but the plight of that woman and the utter helplessness of the entire situation sent a shiver down my spine. That was the moment when I understood that I had to see this through to the end, because even if nothing else was getting exorcised that evening, I had to definitely exorcise the ghosts of my own past memories.

'When is the exorcism?' I asked.

'At 5.30 p.m. It will be conducted by the Mahanta.'

'We have a couple of hours till then,' I said. 'It's all right. I will use the time to mingle with the other devotees and find out what brings them here.'

Vishnu nodded. But he cautioned me to be careful and not reveal my real intent. He suggested that I should also behave like one of the devotees, for only then would they open up to me and share their experiences frankly.

It worked. I went as one of them and engaged in casual conversation with some of the people around. It was a unique experience to say the least; in a way, it felt like being in a hospital waiting room. Almost everyone was suffering from some or the other 'problem' and they were here looking for guidance, and hopefully a cure. I saw a white-haired woman whose eyes wouldn't stay steady. I was told that she was possessed by a hundred ghosts who had attached themselves to her when she walked past a graveyard at night. Another woman was beating the ground with her bare palms and her relatives were just looking on. She was supposed to be a vessel for several spirits too and they had latched on to her because she was—as they put it—'too beautiful'. Her beauty had become her curse.

That was the one thing I noticed these people had in common—all the 'patients', as they were referred to here, were women. I scanned the area to see if there were any men anywhere, but none of them were men. That remained a conundrum—did ghosts only possess women? Or was this another example of the debilitating patriarchy that is such an intrinsic part of our society?

There was groaning and weeping everywhere I turned. I talked to some of the relatives and, although no one spoke to me at length, one thing became abundantly clear—they were all here in the staunch hope that their problems would be solved and they would be able to take their family members back home in much better health.

Their conviction was infectious. The firm belief all of these people had diluted my earlier stance, and now I wanted to know what was really going to happen. All of them looked so different from the usual ailing people. Was there really something inside them that no medicine but only faith could heal?

By the time evening approached, I was completely hooked. In fact, I was now looking forward to witness an exorcism for the second time in my life, and this time I would know better.

———

At exactly 5.30 p.m., the Mahanta strode into the temple, just as I had seen him do years ago. It was not the same person though. This was a different Mahanta, but he had the same forbidding attire and appearance. I was almost at the same spot where I had stood years ago. Vishnu was right next to me. All eyes were turned in the direction of the sanctum sanctorum at the front of the temple. The crowd fell silent as the Mahanta walked in.

A call was made for the patient. There was such an eerie stillness in the hall now that people's breathing could be heard. Upon the call, people's heads turned collectively towards the temple gate. Three figures emerged. The memory tugged at my heart, much as a sharp piece of metal embedded in one's foot would. It was Vishnu's aunt, propped up by two younger temple assistants.

The woman was escorted along the length of the hall. Clearly, she could not walk on her own. She was brought in front of the sanctum sanctorum, where the Mahanta was seated on a small mat placed on the floor. There was another mat in front of him, on which the woman was made to sit.

As the men released their hold on Vishnu's aunt, she looked as if she would fall. There was absolutely no strength in her. I learned from Vishnu that she had been kept on a strict diet of only herbs and berries. The intent was to torture the body so that the ghost inside her would find her body to be an unsuitable vessel and leave.

The Mahanta had a special brass pot used by sadhus, known as a *kamandala*, placed in front of him. Half closing his eyes, he started reciting some mantras. The woman's breathing grew heavy. Soon, her groans became louder than the chief priest's chanting. I could see that the sounds were on account of her feeble physical condition, but the people assembled there had a look of wonder in their eyes. They did not see the woman groaning; they saw it as a sign of the pain felt by the spirit supposed to be dwelling inside her.

Then the chief priest took some water from his kamandala and sprinkled it on the woman's face with great force. The woman, who had not been expecting this, flinched and yelled. The audience gasped. Some of the people in the crowd also began mumbling their god's name as if something very ominous was going to happen.

The Mahanta stopped chanting all of a sudden. He opened his eyes and stared at the woman. Then the questioning began.

'Who are you?'

The woman mumbled a response, but it was inaudible to the rest of us.

'Why are you inside this woman?'

The woman said something, but again, we couldn't hear her.

The Mahanta shouted, 'What? Speak up?'

'I am just a simple woman,' said the lady. 'Please let me go.'

The Mahanta suddenly slapped his knee. 'Aha! So you are a deceiving obstinate one, are you? Stop pretending to be this woman. We all know who you are. I can see your filthy form. Tell me, why are you tormenting her and her family?'

The woman, in great discomfort, said, 'I am not . . .'

'What do you want?' the Mahanta roared.

'I just want . . . I just want to go home . . . Please let me go home . . .' the woman pleaded.

'You unholy preta!' the Mahanta raged on. 'You creature of the underworld! You have no place in this holy land of ours.

Your filth is undesirable. You cannot come to our world and possess innocent people like this lady. You need to be taught a lesson.'

In the audience, the people started chanting louder. Some were cheering the Mahanta now. Some held one another's hands. There were tears in the eyes of the older folk.

'Bring me the baton!' the Mahanta said, trembling with rage.

Another assistant emerged from the crowd. This one was built like a bull. Towering above everyone else in the crowd, people scurried away to let him pass. He came to the space where the Mahanta was and then I saw with rising dread—there was a heavy club in his hands, its tip smeared with some kind of red paste.

'This is your last chance!' the Mahanta said. 'Leave this woman right now.'

Nothing happened. The woman's groaning only rose a pitch.

'Start!' the Mahanta boomed.

Instantly, the bull-like assistant raised the red club and brought it down heavily upon the woman's back.

The woman shot up in pain. Given her heavy build, she could not rise all the way, but she arched up before toppling over, screaming and writhing in agony.

'See this, all of you!' the Mahanta shouted out to the assembled people. 'This is not the woman suffering; this is the preta inside her. Look at the evil one wriggling. It is just one blow, but he has already tasted some of my anger.'

The people hailed the Mahanta as if he had performed a miracle.

I was fuming. I turned to speak to Vishnu.

'Vishnu, the woman is being beaten. Of course she will scream. Where is the preta here?'

Vishnu hushed me.

I was silenced by another shot that rang out. The woman had been beaten again. The Mahanta again made his proclamation. The audience cheered.

This went on another ten or fifteen times, by the end of which the woman was a mangled lump on the floor. The Mahanta stood over her, legs apart, arms akimbo, as if he had vanquished some terrible foe. 'It is a very obstinate preta,' he said. 'I have weakened him today, but he will need more such treatments. Take this woman away and bring her back tomorrow. She will have to appear here for seven days before she is fully treated.'

As Vishnu's aunt was taken away, I heard her say to her family, 'It's all for the good. It's the only way to cure me.'

Those words shook me. And then I understood the bigger part of this faith. The fact that this tradition has continued down the centuries is because the people themselves believe something is wrong with them. There may be no ghost or spirit in her after all, but as long as she is forced to believe it, how could things go another way?

———

Vishnu and I sat with two of his friends who had joined us by now. There was going to be another exorcism that evening and I wished to see that one as well. We sat in silence, sipping tea just outside the temple. We had seen a lot, and it hadn't been easy. Vishnu tried to talk to me intermittently, but I told him that I'd tell him what I thought after we saw the next one.

Soon it was time for the second exorcism. We could tell from the way people pushed en masse into the temple once more. We went through a door at the back of the premises—where the tents were—and stood in the same place as before.

The Mahanta was already in position.

The woman was brought in—yes, no surprises there, it was again a woman—and made to sit on the mat in front of the Mahanta. This was a much-younger woman, and the chief priest introduced her to the crowd as a newlywed bride who had suffered a seizure on her first marital night itself. This was uncharacteristic of him; he had not introduced Vishnu's aunt previously.

He went on to ask her a barrage of questions. I listened intently, because the line of questioning seemed to be somewhat different.

'Who are you?' he began.

The woman grunted. It was a highly inhuman grunt that instantly grabbed my attention.

The Mahanta asked again. There was great severity in his tone.

This time the woman bared her teeth. I am not sure it is possible for a human to do that. It was a canine snarl. The lips curled all the way back to display her teeth—a perfectly white set of healthy dentures.

The audience was really intrigued. I could see the fear lining their foreheads. To be honest, I did not know what to think either. There was no way this woman's reactions were normal. For a moment, I sensed a chill around me. The realization that I was in the middle of an exorcism was upon me now.

'Tell me your name,' the Mahanta said.

The woman rolled her tongue in a highly obscene manner, drool dripping down her lips right up to her chin. She took her tongue in and then said, 'Roopesh'.

At that, the audience almost missed a heartbeat. The voice she had said it in—it was a man's voice.

The Mahanta looked around at the stunned audience as though he had made a great conquest.

'Roopesh!' he repeated. 'From where do you come, Roopesh?'

'Desert . . .' she continued in the man's voice. 'No water.' And then some of the worst expletives I have ever heard issued from her mouth.

The Mahanta was outraged at the cuss words. His eyes grew red and it looked as if he would burst into flames. 'You will behave!' he thundered. 'This is a temple.'

She belted out some more words in response—so abusive that I could not possibly spell them out here.

The chief, now beet-red, asked for his club. 'You are a foul-mouthed evil scum of the earth,' he raged. 'You shall not be allowed to stay here. Your punishment is going to be severe. Brace yourself.'

There was no change in the woman's demeanour, but she played with the collar of the kurta she was wearing. As her fingers lowered the collar, her neck was exposed, and the audience let out a loud gasp. There was a sickly pallor of green on her neck. It looked ghastly.

The bodybuilder assistant brought out the club. The Mahanta gave him an immediate order and the beating began.

This time, the beating was more severe. As she was struck repeatedly, the woman's clothes began to tear, and through the rips in her clothes, scars could be seen. They were scars of some kind of blight that could not be explained.

'These are all marks of the devil,' the Mahanta said. 'She has the devil inside her. But I have control over him. I will cast him out if it is the last thing I do.'

He went into a frenzy after that as he furiously began to chant mantras. He took water from his kamandala and sprinkled it on the woman as he chanted. The woman yelled out louder and louder—these were groans and sighs alternated with a most raucous demonic giggling which was intended to mock the chief. An assistant brought him a couple of small boxes, from which the chief blew two different colours of powders—red and orange—right into the woman's eyes.

In about ten minutes, the floor of the temple had turned red and orange. The woman's back was revealed now and there were some more green scars visible. But other than that, the woman grew still. The groaning and giggling stopped and she lay spread-eagled on the floor.

The Mahanta stood over her. 'Who are you?' he asked, after about a minute of silent meditation.

'Dipali,' she said, this time taking her original name in a girl's voice.

The audience immediately broke out into a cheer. They shouted the Mahanta's name with full gusto.

'Such a powerful demon,' the chief said, 'but this time, I could cast it out in just one sitting. Listen everyone, not all spirits and creatures behave in the same manner. This girl is healed. Her family can take her away.'

The Mahanta held the hem of his dhoti and strode out of the temple in a heroic manner. Behind him, the audience exulted, breaking into a rapturous chanting of the glory of his name.

Everyone started to move out and we walked out too. Vishnu asked me when we were near the temple gates, 'Now what do you think?'

I did not know what to say.

'I don't know!' I said honestly. 'The second case looked genuine to me.'

'Genuine in what sense?'

'As if she might be really possessed.'

Vishnu smiled. 'Then you think this was a real exorcism? Do you think my aunt is possessed too?'

My mind was pervaded by so many thoughts at that moment that it was unfair of him to ask me my opinions right then. The thing about exorcisms is that you cannot tell what is an authentic case and what isn't. I cannot vouch for the Mahanta's genuineness, or the lack of it, but what I saw the second time had me nonplussed.

I bade goodbye and made my way back to the hotel. I saw that Vishnu's faith had been bolstered, whether on account of me, I couldn't say. I didn't tell him anything. He too had started out with scepticism, but it now appeared as if he was considering his aunt's case to have been a real case of possession. As he walked away, I heard him telling his friends that there are some things that cannot be reasoned or explained.

But then something happened when I reached the gates that showed me the truth.

Just outside, I saw the girl again. Dipali. She was in a different dress now, a new, shiny one. She was walking towards a car with a driver waiting for her. The people she was with, supposedly her family, came with her to the car. There they all stopped, and I saw one of those men giving her a bundle of notes. She stuffed them into her dress, waved goodbye and got into the car. Just before being driven away, she took out a pair of swanky sunglasses and put them on.

I was stumped. The woman wasn't at all the demure, newlywed village bride I had seen in the temple. She had become different—so different!

As I walked out of the gate, it hit me. The woman was probably an actor. Everything she did—speaking in a man's voice, the beating, the rips in her dress, even the green scars—all of it could be faked. The money given to her was her fee, and by the thickness of the wad I saw exchange hands, it was a substantial amount.

So, was it that? Had the priests staged a performance to consolidate the position of the temple as one famed for exorcism? By the time I reached my hotel, I was sure that it was just that.

The paranormal world isn't something that reveals itself so openly. From all I have seen and learnt, spirits are shy and they don't come out and interact with humans so freely. They would not show themselves to a large audience in such a manner.

Whether exorcisms are true or not, I cannot opine on that. I am yet to see a real exorcism, but stories of them abound, and some of those come from renowned people in the field. When that happens, you need to think twice about everything.

However, I am sure what I saw at the temple was a sham. I know it was staged for the benefit of the onlookers. My probing tells me that the temple does not take a fee from any of its 'patients' or their families, but that might not really be necessary. It is possible that the temple does it simply to gain a reputation and the donations they receive might be enough for them to carry on this practice.

There, that was the story. I am glad I went and saw things again for myself, because now I don't think about it much. This is something that goes on, and will continue to go on, and we cannot do much to stop it. As long as these beliefs are so firmly entrenched in the minds of the masses, one man can do only so much to make people see it for what it is.

Epilogue

So, we have come to the end of this journey. And if you have followed me thus far, I can presume that, through the ten stories in this book, you have come to know me and my beliefs. That was my primary purpose in compiling my adventures with the paranormal world in this book. I wanted you to see what I have seen, even though you might not be able to visit all these places.

The process of writing this book was quite straightforward. I met my co-author, Neil D'Silva, and over a long interview in his writing room, he tried to understand me as a person. We then got to discussing my adventures, and I shared with him not only what I encountered at these locations but also my mental state at the most pivotal points of the journey. He was more interested in my perceptions of the phenomena in these places, rather than what had really happened—and that is what he has brought out in this book. Neil then wove these conversations into stories. Throughout the process, we had multiple discussions. We wanted the stories to be as authentic as possible, and for nothing to be lost in translation. That was important to us, as we didn't want to merely give you tales to read on a long lonesome night; we wanted the takeaway to be profound as well.

And those are the lessons I learned, the beliefs I accumulated along the way.

Let me put that to you in one simple question. *Do I believe in ghosts?* This is what I am asked everywhere, no exceptions. And my answer is this: Yes, there is a life beyond what we can see. I believe in the soul, and I believe in the immortality of the soul until it attains salvation, as per Hindu beliefs. I also believe that there are times and situations, such as after death, where this soul finds itself homeless, that is, without a body. On these occasions, the soul might manifest itself in different forms, at times even physical. And that might be the root of all the paranormal phenomena that we encounter in our dimension.

But where are these souls when they are not in their bodies, that is, when their corporal vessels are dead? Do they float around? Do they go and gather in places where no other sentient organism visits, which is why some locations are believed to be haunted? I will not profess to have a great deal of knowledge on this, but I can say: Yes, there are places which these between-world entities inhabit. I have had experiences with a few of them, such as, most notably, in the abandoned village of Kuldhara, and in the car outside Vas Villa. But that is all I can say. Yet when you are in these places, you can get a sense of something being 'not normal'. Now whether that is 'paranormal' or not is a question that cannot be answered easily.

What I found, by and large, is that the danger that humans pose is always greater than that presented by any possible ghosts or other kinds of supernatural entities. I saw this in Bhangarh, and I saw this at the temple where I saw the sham exorcism rites. I witnessed it at the Sonpur Bhoot Mela as well, where it is unscrupulous men who deceive gullible folk and give rise to frightening stories that aren't true. In my experience, the human factor, rather than any supernatural cause, contributes much more towards lending a place the reputation for being haunted.

Please bear with me as I share this with you: In India, the pervasiveness of black magic and superstition is so deep that it causes an alarming number of deaths every year. Check out the newspapers. Not those in the urban metros, but those in the smaller towns and cities of our country. You will find people committing suicides and killing others on the pretext of some superstitious belief or other. Fake ascetics are all around us, but what's more dangerous is the number of people who believe in them. These are the susceptible folk, people who can be easily persuaded to kill themselves or others under the guise of some flimsy occult notion.

This is what I want you to know, my main purpose behind writing this book. Whether there are ghosts or not is a matter of debate. As our knowledge of the universe expands, I hope we shall eventually have a definitive answer. But the fact that stands undisputed today is that black magic and superstition are very much prevalent among us. They are deceiving people and playing with their lives. This is what we have to understand. This is why I am trying to get to the bottom of paranormal science, especially the way it is in India. Through my adventures, I am only trying to learn what really exists, even if it is hidden from us today, and the facade that is created by deceptive people to make a quick buck at the expense of others' faith and beliefs.

I hope this journey has been of some value to you.

Jay Alani

Acknowledgements

Jay Alani:

A person who sets out on an unconventional journey and achieves a modest degree of success has many people to thank. As I present this book to you, the first book with my name on the cover, I wish to express my thankfulness to the people who brought me here.

My first mention of gratitude goes to my parents—my father, Narayan Das Alani, and my mother, Asha Alani. They have always been my strongest pillars of strength. Even without knowing the nature of the journey that I was going to embark on, and despite the fact that I lived away from home for long periods of time, they have showered upon me their unstinted support and faith.

I also thank, from the depths of my heart, the love of my life, Priyanka Singh. She has been the unflinching light in my times of darkness, always standing by my side and getting me to keep going. I thank her for keeping her faith in me, for trying to understand my passion and for aiding me in following that passion. She is one of the few individuals in my life who has stood by me, and for me, even as I faced social taboos in my line of work.

My utmost thanks to the voice of my stories in this book, the scribe to my narrative sketches, Neil D'Silva. He has worked with the utmost passion and enhanced the accounts with his crisp storytelling skills, making them a pleasure to read, while, at the same time, retaining the factual accuracy of the tales. I thank our publishers, Penguin Random House India, and our commissioning editor, Gurveen Chadha, for investing their faith in these stories and bringing them to the world. It takes a far-sighted publisher of immense stature to see value in what we have to offer you.

I reserve the largest chunk of my gratitude to a person with great vision—Suhail Mathur, of our literary agency, the Book Bakers. It was his idea to make this book happen and he worked with great enthusiasm to ensure everything fell into place. That you are able to read our work today is largely due to his efforts.

Being a paranormal investigator isn't easy. Getting access to locations, scouting for required permissions, making contacts with the necessary people—these are uphill tasks and they often pose impediments in the progress of our journey. Hence, I thank every security guard posted at the locations I have hunted, the authorities who have given their permission, the people who have given me leads and the people who have followed me on my missions. None of these stories would have been possible without them.

Finally, I thank all the people who have helped me professionally by giving me the space to talk about my beliefs and convictions. I thank all my TEDx talk organizers, my podcast presenters and the hosts of *Haunted Talks* for providing me their platforms. I thank each and every member of the audience, the people who follow me on social media and everyone who has ever spared even a moment to listen to or read my words. It is because of your strength that I keep moving forward to pursue my vision of shattering blind beliefs in this world we live in.

Neil D'Silva:

If it takes an entire village to raise a child, then it takes the entire world to raise an author. Everyone and everything shapes an author's pliable mind, filling it with enough grist to form his stories and skills to deliver them. I take the opportunity here to thank those who have brought me up to this point and who now look forward to seeing me grow further.

I begin by thanking my father, Philip D'Silva, who filled—nay, flooded—the house with books, and my mother, Leena D'Silva, who taught me to read them. I thank my brother, Roy D'Silva, who takes particular joy in criticizing my stories; he doesn't know that his criticism is what eggs me on to write better.

I would not have taken to writing at all without my wife Anita's near-coercion and enthusiasm to see my name displayed on store shelves. I also thank our children, Gilmore and Felicia, for giving me the space to write.

I fondly remember the day I met my co-author, Jay Alani, for the first time. We gelled together within the first few minutes, and he shared tales of his paranormal exploits with me. He let me into his world and allowed me to understand him as a person, which made this a much better book. It is his humble and frank approach that made writing this book an unmitigated pleasure.

I thank our publishers at Penguin Random House India who found this book worthy enough to be published. Our commissioning editor, Gurveen Chadha, is a writer's dream editor. She, along with her team, patiently assisted us through the intricate processes of crafting and designing this book. I laud their editing skills.

I am grateful to the friends of my childhood—in the Bachani Nagar society of Malad East, Mumbai, where I grew up, and those from my school, Children's Academy—who eagerly lent me their ears when I told them my stories. Their patient listening precipitated my genesis as a horror storyteller. I thank one of my teachers in particular, Mr V. Mukundan, who taught me English in class ten, who challenged me with different topics to write on and introduced me to various competitions where I could hone my storytelling skills.

I thank all my readers, of both this work and my past works, and especially those who have spared a moment to leave me a review or speak about it in any manner. For an author, the knowledge that he has readers out there is the biggest blessing.

I saved my thanks for the biggest contributor to shape this book for the last. This is for Suhail Mathur of our literary agency, the Book Bakers, without whom this book would not have taken flight at all. The book itself was his idea, and he was instrumental in introducing me to Jay Alani. Suhail has been the man Friday of my literary career so far and continues to be. Words aren't enough to acknowledge the conviction he has in my writing and the magnanimity he has shown to me.

Our work is now in your hands, dear readers, and I thank each and every one of you for taking the time to read our book.

A Note on the Authors

JAY ALANI is a paranormal investigator whose idea of fun is to spend a night at a reputedly haunted location, all alone. He has explored over sixty haunted locations in India and investigated over 130 individual cases of unexplained phenomena. He has been on several TEDx platforms and is known for his *Haunted Talks*. He hosts a podcast, *Paranormal Reality*, on Hubhopper, and is soon slated to host podcasts on Gaana and Storytel. Jay aspires to crusade against superstitious beliefs and blind faith in India and unearth the real truth behind paranormal activities.

Jay hails from Patna and currently lives in New Delhi. This is his debut book.

 NEIL D'SILVA is an author with a proclivity for the horror genre. He quit a teaching career of eighteen years and made the shift into full-time writing at the age of forty. Success came to him when his debut novel, *Maya's New Husband*, hit #1 on the Amazon.in bestseller list, in the horror category. Since then he has been placed on several lists featuring Indian horror novelists. He gives back to the writing and reading community of India through his annual litfest, Litventure. Neil has spoken on the TEDx platform and has also conducted writing workshops at esteemed institutions such as IIT Kanpur.

Neil lives in Mumbai with his wife, Anita, and their two children, Gilmore and Felicia.